PRAISE FOR WINE FOR ROSES

"*Wine for Roses* is a lushly written novella full of intriguing magic and love of all kinds. The plot blooms amid a slow-burning romance. The characters are complex, and I enjoyed getting to know them."
—**E. H. Lupton, author of the *Wisconsin Gothic* series**

"Such a clever queer take on *Beauty and the Beast* in a modern, midwestern font… a thoughtful, fantastic escape from the mundane, a mental side-step into what may be stirring just beyond the next field of grain."
—**Amanda Cherry, author of the *Ruby Killingsworth* series**

"One of the most endearing versions of *Beauty and the Beast* that I've ever read. Tender and hopeful. A balm for my garden-loving heart!"
—**Meredith Rose, author of the *Ladies of Baker Street* and *Alchemy Empire* series**

WINE FOR ROSES

EMILY O'MALLEY LIU

Published by Shiraki Press
Mill Creek, Washington, USA
First edition 2026

For information about this book, including distribution and media reviews, scan or visit:

shirakipress.com/books/wine-for-roses/

WINE FOR ROSES
Copyright © 2026 by Emily O'Malley Liu
All rights reserved.

ISBN: 978-1-970458-05-3 (Paperback)
ISBN: 978-1-970458-03-9 (EPUB)

This book is a work of fiction. Names, characters, organizations, places, and events are products of the author's imagination, or are used fictitiously. Any resemblance to actual persons, living or dead, is entirely coincidental.

NO PART OF THIS BOOK MAY BE USED OR REPRODUCED TO TRAIN ARTIFICIAL INTELLIGENCE SYSTEMS.

Library of Congress Control Number: 2026934851

Published by Shiraki Press
P.O. Box 13394, Mill Creek, WA 98082
shirakipress.com

To Saka. This one was always for you.

The stolen rose blooms best.

—folk wisdom

ONE

MY FATHER WAS a rose rustler. The early seasons of my life were measured in the lifecycles of rose bushes, and I memorized David Austin's catalogue of English roses the way other little boys memorize the makes of cars. He liked to quiz me as we walked through the garden that eventually overtook our entire property. Evelyn, Queen of Sweden, Scepter D'Isle—these were the aristocratic names that colored my early memories of that otherwise utterly unremarkable house, my only home for twenty-four years.

It was raining the night my father came home carrying a single stem of an ordinary Madame Alfred Carrière. He deposited the pale pink noisette in my hands and shucked off his windbreaker, as soaked as the rose.

I cradled it on instinct. My father handled cut roses with impartial expertise. I held each blossom like a broken butterfly. "Any luck?"

He grunted instead of answering and went upstairs. After a few minutes I heard the shower running. He'd be up there for a while. Some people went for a run to de-stress. My father showered, running up a water bill we couldn't afford.

But my question had been semi-rhetorical in any case. My father had gone that afternoon to visit a property he learned about on a tip from a local, while making a delivery of bouquets to a supermarket outside Indianapolis. A rose rustler's objective was to find those hidden old garden gems, uncatalogued by the modern rose trade, grown wild and forgotten on somber old estates. If he had come home carrying a single stem of a variety I could name on sight, then the trip had clearly been a failure.

When my father came back down, I cracked him a beer and turned on the White Sox game. He gave me a half-smile of exhausted gratitude as he sank onto the cracked leather of the BarcaLounger. The Sox were up one-nothing, bottom of the third.

"Want another?" I asked when the inning ended.

He shook his head, tucked the empty can into the cushions, and looked at me skeptically. "I know you're not watching the game."

I lifted the rose. "What's up with this?"

The TV blared a commercial for dishwasher pods—so clean your dishes will sparkle! My father switched it off. "I stole it."

"You stole a rose?" My father's career was an unorthodox one that involved scavenging old estates, but he wasn't a thief. "You didn't let them know you'd be looking in the gardens?"

"It was abandoned," he said shortly. "Or I thought it was. You know what Ethan, I will have another, thanks."

I laid the Madame on the coffee table and went to get another beer from the fridge.

My father was a rose rustler, but he was not a very successful one. He had never come across that Black Swan varietal that might make him sought-after in the rose world, that might allow him to devote himself full time to his rose business. The rose that might have meant we could stop living off the insufficient income from our grocery store bouquet sales. Worrying about water bills and buying cheap beer.

"A damn Madame Alfred Carrière." My father took the can from me and rubbed his hand across his forehead. "I don't know what came over me."

He was upset, which made me anxious. I curled my fingers against my knee, fighting the urge to take his hand in mine like I did when I was a kid. "What happened?"

He dropped his hand into his lap and sighed again. "The place was overgrown, clearly empty. No cars in the drive, no lights on in any of the windows. Big place. I knocked on the front door and hollered, just to be sure. I went around back hoping there was still a garden. And there was." His face creased, and his voice turned wondering. "There must have been thousands of bushes, dozens of varietals, maybe hundreds. And they were all old garden roses, not a goddamn hybrid tea in sight. But it was run wild, hadn't been pruned in ages. Shoots in all directions, lotsa dead wood hanging around. And nothing blooming. Not so much as a bud."

"But..." I looked at the bloom on the coffee table.

My father shrugged helplessly. "There was this garden folly. I think it was supposed to be a Greek temple. Very Victorian, you know. It had a bench, with an arch above it, a rose trained over one side. A centerpiece. I'd've sworn there wasn't a bud on the damn thing when I first looked at it but I turned around and—there it was."

"And you took it."

"I took it. I was just—it was so strange, the way it just appeared. It was like it was meant for me. We need new pruners, by the way. I dropped my No. 2s and forgot to grab them before I left."

It was unlike my father to be forgetful, and that worried me. His description of the rose was also downright bizarre. The best rosarians were hedge witches like my father. His magic allowed his roses to bloom softly through scorching heatwaves, helped dormant canes survive frigid Midwest winters, and kept disease in check. The plants took on a beautiful shape for my father. But I had never seen one bloom on his command.

"There was a garden house too. Creepy place, all covered in dead vines. But it was a decent size, a bungalow, and I thought, maybe it'll have a hose bib. There was a spigot on the outside of the house, and I used it to wet a cloth to wrap the stem in. That's what I was doing when he found me."

"Who?"

"The trustee. That's what he called himself. Accused me of stealing his roses. Well, I guess I had stolen his roses." The words settled into the space between us, floating slowly towards the coffee table until they lit upon the Madame. "I told him who I was, what I was doing—I had a card on me, so I gave it to him. I told him about the business, about you."

He inhaled sharply but then didn't continue, staring down at his hands with a deeply creased brow. A thousand scenarios coursed through my mind, each worse than the last—the police summoned, lawsuits filed. More problems we couldn't afford.

"Did he threaten you?"

"He offered me a job. Said he wanted help in the garden. Looking for a full-time rosarian for the season, someone to bring the garden back to a respectable state."

That was unexpected. I sat back, stunned. Three months poking around an old garden sounded like my father's idea of paradise. "How much?"

He hesitated, then nodded. "Thirty."

"How many hours is he looking for?"

"Not thirty an hour. Thirty grand. For the whole job."

Thirty thousand dollars. It was enough to eliminate the medical debt that had hung over our lives ever since mom got sick. The debt that kept my father stuck selling bland bouquets of hybrid teas to grocery stores. The debt over which I had quit college to help keep the business afloat. I'd never gone back. There wasn't any money.

"Dad, do it."

My father shook his head. "No—I can't. I have the business to run, and—"

"The hell with the business." I stood up, and my voice rose with me. "Do it. You could go back to rose rustling full time, quit the grocery circuit."

My father looked down at his hands again. He was still the tall, powerfully built man I had traipsed after in my childhood, the man who wrangled five-gallon buckets of water and spades of clay soil for a living. It was sometimes hard to remember he was also a man living with MS, a chronic disease that had flared up late in life and which sometimes made everyday tasks difficult.

He *couldn't* do it. Our own rose farm, from which we grew the commercially appealing roses we sold to grocery stores around the county, consisted only of what we could fit in our backyard, but it was already too much for him alone. He looked small suddenly, curled into the recliner like a child. A battered rose.

"I can do it," I said.

My father looked up. "No—I'm serious, Ethan. We're talking about an acre of abandoned garden. It would take one man all season."

"Then I'll be there all season. Our pruning is done. You can do without me well enough. Maybe I can come home on the weekends to help out with the rest."

He shook his head. "The roses—he wants them to bloom. It's already June. There isn't a chance."

My father knew roses. If he thought a garden was doomed, it probably was. "What did you tell him?"

"That I'd be back in a week, give him an answer then. And pay for the Madame Alfred Carrière stem. He didn't have a phone. Odd character."

"The Madame bloomed. It can't be hopeless." I moved towards the stairs. "I'm going to shower."

My father didn't move. "It's for you."

I paused with my hand on the banister. "What is?"

He nodded at the rose still lying on the coffee table. "The Madame. He said to give it to you."

THE NEXT MORNING it was still raining hard.

Rainy days weren't days off on a rose farm—we still had plenty to do in the shelter of the house, wrapping grocery store bundles and making phone calls—but on days with poor weather, we took the mornings a little slower.

That particular rainy morning, I had taken a favorite book from my shelf but couldn't focus and instead sat staring out at the gray light that filtered in through my window. The Madame Alfred Carrière loomed out of an old jelly jar of water on my desk.

The Madame was one of the best-known old garden roses, beautifully fragrant, its cupped white petals so fluffy it was practically indecent. Most often, the blooms tinted towards pale pink near the centers. This one seemed a bit pinker than most. But weather could affect petal color. Perhaps it was the rain.

We had no Madame specimen on our property. But I trusted my father's assessment. Arthur Keating had the uncanny ability to identify any varietal, even when not in bloom. Before she died, my mother loved to challenge him—blindfold him and pass him a cutting to identify by touch and scent alone. He was always right. As a child, I thrilled to watch what for them passed for romance.

Most years, my father's symptoms prevented him from working for at least a few weeks. On the days when walking was difficult for him, my mother and I would do the pruning and the watering and the harvesting, wrapping the thorny bouquets with an efficiency born of years of experience, not magic. My mother used to tell me that we were the horsepower to my father's talent. I would tell her she was too beautiful to be a horse, and she would laugh and laugh.

When we lost her, we became a family of two. I wanted to protect him, the way that he had protected me as a child. My father applied for disability when his symptoms got worse, and I took care of the business. It was good enough for me. I hadn't fit in at IU Bloomington, in any case—the quiet gay kid with dirt under his fingernails and a father with a career no one had ever heard of. People think they're interested in roses, but they don't actually want to hear about the reality of it—the pruning and the spraying and the soil amendments. Even my father's magical affinity for roses was too subtle to be very entertaining. I'd watched enough people's eyes glaze over, back when I was still trying, a little, to make people think I was interesting.

A bang from downstairs jolted me out of bed and had me running down the stairs two at a time.

"Dad?"

"Don't run so fast." He scowled at me, worried. He was standing at the old range in the kitchen, the cast iron already heating in front of him. "Thought I'd make breakfast. We still have eggs, right?"

I sighed and grabbed the carton from the refrigerator. Breakfast in our house was usually a milk-and-cereal affair, or maybe jelly-and-toast when we were feeling fancy. He was showing off, showing me that his symptoms were under control.

I made coffee while he cracked eggs into the pan,

heaping three scoops of cheap coffee grounds into the ancient percolator. Once it began to drip, I turned back to him. "I don't want to argue," I started, but he waved me off.

"Don't. We don't have to talk about that now. Let's just enjoy a nice breakfast." He slid a large helping of underdone scrambled eggs onto a plate and handed it to me.

My father and I never argued, we merely disagreed, and then whoever decided they were in the wrong simply capitulated without apology. I took the plate and slid into the booth, the one he had built when my mother said she wanted a breakfast nook. The back of the house faced the roses, and the bay window had a lovely view. He built it to custom-fit the little oddly shaped corner in our kitchen. We rarely used it since Mom died. Most of the time we just ate in front of the TV.

"So, you going out tonight?"

I looked up at him curiously.

"It's Friday," he supplied.

"Oh." I picked at my eggs. "No."

"What about Caitlyn? I thought the two of you liked going out to that—you know, that place in Indy."

I smiled. "You can say gay bar, Dad."

He rolled his eyes. "You should be out with friends on a Friday night. You're twenty-four, it's not normal to be cooped up at home."

"I like it here." It had been months since I last went out with friends. No—it was over a year, now that I thought about it. I tried for a while after I left college. Reconnected with friends from high school, gotten a group together and gone out. It was fun, until it wasn't. People moved away, transferred to colleges on the East Coast. Caitlyn got married last year, and she and her husband had a baby. I didn't see her anymore, except via photos on social media.

"You sure you feeling alright? If you feel any—"

"I'm fine," I said. "Really. Thanks for breakfast." I scraped the rest of my eggs onto his plate.

"You hardly ate anything."

"You made six eggs for two people." I patted my stomach, and my father frowned. He always thought I ought to have eaten more than I did, like he and his cousins when they were my age. While I'd inherited his Irishman's height, the fact remained that I was half Mexican and therefore a normal human, unlike the giants on his side. "I had plenty."

"Where are you going?"

"Hardware store. We need new pruners." I grabbed the keys from the bowl on the side table. "Anything else you want?"

He shook his head. "It's raining. The roads will be a mess. Ethan—"

"I'll take an umbrella." I let the porch door slam behind me before he could say anything else.

I was lonely. I knew I was lonely, but talking about it didn't make it better. I had chosen the things that were the most important to me. The business and my father. If finding my people had to be put on the back burner for a little while, then so be it. I refused to regret prioritizing the things I loved.

I took an umbrella and the pink truck, the one I thought of as my truck after Dad bought the second one, back when I was first learning to drive. It wasn't really pink of course, just so old that the red paint had faded summer after summer until it became unfair to call it red any longer. Even the newer truck, painted a more sensible white, was a bit dinged. Nothing in our house was new anymore.

The Home Depot parking lot was packed, and I had to circle three times. A trio of men stood by the entrance to the lot, their faces shaded under baseball caps. The third time I passed, one of them looked up, eyes bright in his dark face. I wondered if any of them were hedge witches.

I made my way to the garden center. The rack that sported gardening tools in various sizes and brands stretched the entire aisle. Every rosarian needs a pair of Felco No. 2 pruners for deadheading and pruning, and the ones my father lost had been less than a year old, just recently replaced. Good pruners should last for decades. They weren't cheap.

It was still drizzling, which made the outdoor section feel like a rainforest, or what I had imagined as a kid that a rainforest would feel like. Most home improvement stores didn't sell the type of roses that my father and I grew—if you wanted specialty roses you needed to patronize a proper rose farm—but even the Home Depot garden center had all sorts of plants, and I loved them all. Mums and lilacs, impatiens and daffodils. Seasonals and perennials, change and constancy. Plants didn't care how you dressed or what you had to say as long as you came with a watering can and maybe some fertilizer. They didn't know that my father had relapsing-remitting MS, the symptoms of which came and went in flares, and that I pruned them when he couldn't. Plants had no expectations. They never wanted more than you could give.

The associate behind the counter hummed as she rang

me up. She was a large, cheerful woman with silver-blonde hair and a collection of silver bangles up both wrists. They made music as she scanned the pruners. She smiled and held them up.

"Do you grow roses?"

"Yes," I responded. "Home farm."

"I have a cousin who grows roses. Weeds don't dare grow in her garden. Would you call that magic?" Her eyes lit up as she scanned my face hopefully, as if looking for some sort of sign that would identify me as a hedge witch.

I shrugged, took my receipt, and ducked back out into the rain.

When I got home, my father was still on his feet, whistling and cleaning up the range with vinegar and an old rag. I wondered if he had jumped up from the table when he heard the truck pull up the drive.

I unwrapped the new pruners and set them on the table.

"Great, great," he said cheerfully.

I frowned. My father was not the kind of person who feigned cheerfulness. "Dad—"

"I've decided to do it."

"You've—what?"

"The gardening job, at the estate." He flung the rag across the room so that it landed in the laundry basket, which I had been meaning to take down to the basement. "I'm going to take it."

"Dad—"

"I feel strong enough, I really do. I've been in remission for months."

My frustration couldn't withstand the onslaught of his cheerfulness, and I felt myself deflate. "You've been great,

Dad," I said carefully. "But it makes more sense for me to go. You need to run the business."

That was a lie, and we both knew it. I was perfectly capable of running the rest of the summer by myself. The business was not the problem. But if my father was out on this one estate all summer, even if he stayed in remission, he would have to give up an entire season of rose rustling. Another year lost, without finding that long-forgotten rose he could re-cultivate and sell.

My father shook his head. "You shouldn't be trapped on a lonely estate all summer. Hell, you shouldn't be trapped here all summer, you should be out and about, having fun." He waved his hands as if to indicate the sort of frivolity in which I, a young person, ought to be indulging. "Your mother would never forgive me for doing this to you."

"You aren't doing anything to me," I said, "and Mom would know that. She did know that. I want to be here." I slid back into the breakfast nook. "Neither of us needs to go. We're getting by"—another lie—"and we'll figure it out together. We always do."

He smiled, but it was sad and small. "There's more, Ethan. That I haven't told you, I mean. About… you know."

I did. "About the money."

He slipped into the nook opposite me, but kept his eyes on the table in between us. "I took a loan out on the business."

"What bank was willing to lend us money?"

"Wasn't a bank." He picked at the threadbare placemat in front of him. Blue and white stripes, the sort of cheerful item you'd expect to find in a happy home. "I borrowed the money from Kay."

The words hit me like a shovel to the gut. My Aunt Kay was my father's younger sister. She still lived up in South Bend and was more like a stern and unloving former teacher than an aunt, a ferocious woman who'd always been disappointed in our family. First when her brother went into farming and then again when I refused to go to Notre Dame. A pair of disappointments.

We'd had a series of larger expenses this year. The battery in my truck had died last month, and the HVAC had given out at the start of the summer. The new pruners I'd bought today.

"What sort of terms did she give you?"

"She didn't." My father grimaced. Kay would be only too happy to lord it over him, her generosity to her poor brother and nephew. We were barely making the hospital payments. If we had Kay to pay back on top of everything else, we may as well go under.

"You have to let me go, Dad," I said. He started to shake his head, but I plowed on. "Look, I can get the work done there as much as possible, then come back here on weekends. It'll be manageable."

"It's a full time job. I doubt you'd be able to take so much as a day off. Ethan, the place was a mess. Dead wood and rot and—"

"I can handle it."

"I know you can." He sighed, but there was pride in the sound. He folded his hands over the pruners on the table and nodded. "I know you can, and you're as stubborn as your mother was. Alright, fine. Go."

"If there's anything you need," I said, "I'll come straight home."

He waved a hand. "Kay's only an hour away. Lord knows she'll be only too happy to come charging in on a white horse."

The Madame Alfred Carrière remained on the desk in my room for six days, its beauty frozen in perfect bloom, lasting on and on like Maccabean oil. It never so much as dropped a petal or developed a brown spot. The morning I left, it finally shattered.

TWO

"BE GOOD," WAS all my father said before I hopped in the pink pickup and headed down US 31. The estate was an hour or so from our part of suburbia, in the middle of nowhere, which in central Indiana meant between one cornfield and another. The drive was made longer by the many miles of unchanging landscape, broken only by the large wind farm just north of Indianapolis, where the white turbines turned steady and relentless in the wide blue Indiana sky.

The estate wasn't on the GPS, and so my father gave me the same instructions he'd received from the client who'd tipped him off. An exit onto a two-lane road led deeper into the windmills, then another turn onto a smaller, poorly maintained road sent the truck bouncing. The next turn wasn't a road at all. No more than a service path for tractors and other machinery, the slice of semi-packed dirt just wide enough for the truck and indistinguishable from all the other service paths I had passed. But this one had a red mailbox at the turnoff.

I passed a split rail fence, which opened up into what I thought at first was a fallow field and then realized was a lawn. A wildly overgrown lawn, with grasses that came up nearly to the tops of the wheels of the truck. Then the road became a pebbled drive, guarded at intervals by gnarled oaks that might have once been stately, but had long since devolved into the fey. Heavily leaf-laden arms reached down to meet the tall grass where it met the edge of the drive.

At the end of the drive was a house.

No wonder my father had sought roses here. The house had the charisma evinced only by houses built before living memory. A mid-Victorian, perhaps, with all the overwrought sentimentality of the era. The facade was all crumbling stones and dead vines and French chimneys. It made no concessions to proportion, winding itself upward unevenly with windows wherever it thought they would do and porticos overlooking the sentry oaks at odd angles. I loved it.

I parked the truck out front and grabbed my duffel from the back seat. The gravel crunched beneath my feet as I wandered up to the house, remarkably free of the weeds that choked the old oaks. The front porch had Virginia creeper grown up and over the railing right up to the massive front door, but the wooden boards felt sturdy and made no noise under my boots.

My knock at the door went unanswered. I hesitated. My father had not entered the main house—he had encountered the trustee near the garden house. Was it trespassing to enter a property to which you had—technically—sort of—been hired?

But I figured it made as much sense to start with the main house as anywhere else. I dropped my duffel and leaned my shoulder into the door. It came more easily than I would have expected given its massive size. It opened onto a foyer, which was dark and cool. Faint light trickled in through a grisaille glass window above the door, glinting dully off an empty chandelier. A staircase wrapped around on itself, disappearing into a dark upper story.

"Hello?" I hollered.

The dust in the air glittered. It swirled, still agitated from my entry, and led off to the left, and I followed an open doorway to a kind of drawing room. A grand piano stood in the center covered with a yellowed drop cloth. When I was a child we had had a neighbor with a small spinet in her living room, and she let me come over after school to practice. My mother had always said I would be better suited for guitar with the callouses on my fingertips already pre-installed. But I loved the delicacy of the piano, its responsiveness. It had been years since I had touched a keyboard.

I lifted one end of the cloth. I expected it to be dusty, but it wasn't. Whatever my father's impression, it was clear that *someone* lived in the house. The windows let in daylight, which bounced off a large upright mirror leant up against the wall behind the piano, positioned so that a person seated at the bench could check their posture. I caught a glimpse of myself, a slouched and uncertain creature huddled over the beautiful instrument. I turned away.

The music room led to a parade of other rooms filled with cloth-covered furniture. A formal living room, a library, two different dining rooms, a billiard room, and finally, near the back of the house, an old-fashioned kitchen. One room opened up to another without hallways, like the house in the game of Clue.

"Colonel Mustard in the kitchen with the candlestick," I muttered, dragging my finger across the curiously clean butcher-block top of a large chef's table. Just off the kitchen was a butler's pantry lined with cabinets surrounding a French door that let in a subtle sunlight. A dumbwaiter hung along the back wall. A big one, large enough that I could almost have crawled inside like Harriet the Spy. Inside the dumbwaiter was a tray spread with cold honeyed ham, several kinds of cheese, and a marvelous loaf of French bread, as well as two different kinds of jam and honey. The bread was warm to the touch.

I called out again, but there was no response. My shoulders clenched with tension, sure of being caught out any minute. The lunch, after all, had to belong to someone. Then I spotted a watering can tucked into a small cubby by the door, gardening gloves folded neatly over the side. A pair of high-quality pruning shears sat next to the can—a pair of No. 2s I recognized as my father's. The pair he had dropped at the estate. Was it all for the expected gardener?

"Thank you," I said uncertainly. The butler's pantry had a curious sentience to it, and I half expected it to respond. It seemed rude, at any rate, not to acknowledge it.

I had the sense the room was proud of itself to have been able to provide such service. But also that it was largely guessing at what sorts of tools a rosarian might need. "You did very well," I reassured it. "A good butler knows his clients."

My stomach rumbled, and I eyed the food hungrily. I could only imagine how it would seem if the trustee found me eating his lunch. After a glance over my shoulder into the kitchen, I snagged a piece of cheese marbled with jam. It tasted a little like pomegranate.

By the time I came back around to the foyer, I had encountered no one. And my duffel, which I was sure I had left on the front porch, was gone. I went out to my truck to make sure I was not misremembering, but the bed held nothing but my tools. I looked back at the house with its massive, intimidating doors. The butler's pantry had an entrance, and there might be others. I must have simply missed someone, crossed paths as I was exploring the house. Perhaps my employer himself, though the state of the house suggested the presence of at least a cleaning crew and perhaps a cook. Did old homes like these still have servants? Perhaps they had taken my duffel to wherever I was meant to stay. I dug through the supplies in the bed of my truck and pulled out a flashlight.

The rooms of the upper story were dark, arranged along a short hallway that wrapped in on itself, a sort of deformed cursive L that quit halfway around. My flashlight glinted off ornate gold sconces and heavy framed portraits of serious-looking Victorian Hoosiers. The sconces had old-fashioned electric bulbs.

As I rounded the little bend, one door stood slightly ajar. It was a bedroom, tall-ceilinged and narrow with a wooden four-poster bed across from a fireplace framed by a cherry wood mantel. At the foot of the bed was my duffel bag. I spun around, looking for whoever had delivered it.

"Hello?"

My voice echoed down the hall. Perhaps whoever it was was deaf and could not hear to respond. It was as likely an explanation as any, but the uncanny absence of my host nevertheless made me uneasy.

The guest room was stuffy but comfortable. The four-poster bed was high enough to warrant the use of the little step stool positioned beside the frame. A princess bed, an absolutely absurd amenity for someone who was, at best, the hired help. A full-length mirror leaned against the wall, less warped than those I had seen downstairs. I ignored it too. The walls were covered in a horrendous floral paper that ran stripes from floor to ceiling. An en suite bathroom was next to the fireplace, and a small French door led out to an inset balcony at the far end. I stepped outside. A stone balustrade came up to my lowest ribs.

From there, I had my first view of the gardens. It was a walled garden laid out in an old English style, with rooms demarcated by box hedges and dominated by large arches designed to hold climbing roses. In another life it must have been quite the spectacle, all color and elegant footpaths. But its edges had run like a watercolor, sending out canes and blind shoots in all directions and overtaking the paths. It made sense why the gardener had been assigned this room. The gardens were visible not just for what they were but for what they should have been. I could see the way the roses and hedges and gravel ought to have cooperated and delineated space. It was a map.

I leaned forward over the balustrade and peered around the wall of the house, which jutted out, blocking my view of the east edge of the gardens. A small bungalow stood at the far corner. From the single chimney emanated a thin slip of smoke, which caught in the wind and blew towards the main house.

I lifted my phone out of my pocket to take a picture, meaning to use it as an actual map, but then I saw that my phone had no service and the battery life was already halfway gone. I switched it to airplane mode and reluctantly slid it back into my jeans. Despite the electric sconces I had seen no outlets anywhere in the house. If I wanted to charge my phone I would have to sit in my truck and waste gas. If I needed to reach my father I'd have to drive back out to the main road. My chest clenched.

I fell back on my heels and folded my arms across my chest against the oncoming wind. At this point I was blatantly putting off facing my new employer. I turned around and marched back into the room. I faced the floor-length mirror reluctantly.

I looked like a gardener, unkempt and windburned. My jeans were stained at the knees from so many hours of kneeling in the dirt and grass, evidence that no laundry detergent could remove. The button-down I had chosen, my newest, was five years old and looked it. I'd inherited my mother's dark hair, and it was long overdue for a haircut, curling around my ears and falling past my collar. The lamps paused in their humming and held their breath, as though the room was awaiting my judgement. I briefly debated tucking in my shirt.

"No point in pretending to be something I'm not," I said.

I sensed the room was disappointed.

IN THE TIME it took to walk downstairs, the sky went from gray to nearly black. I stepped out onto the back porch from the butler's pantry, smelling rain in the air and wishing I had grabbed a jacket. Overhead stretched an elliptical treillage arch over which grew green vines—not roses, but what looked like maybe bleeding heart. A flagstone path stretched out ahead of me, and it beckoned around a bend.

I slipped into the garden and everything else slipped away. I was no longer somewhere in Indiana, between one cornfield and another, but in the British countryside. Box hedges and low stone walls demarcated open-air rooms that rambled easily from one to the next, a gentle maze that urged the itinerant onward. The garden was silent. The kind of silence that means the birds and insects have flown home to roost, and all the small rodents and other creatures have gone to ground ahead of a storm. The smell of the garden rose up around me as I walked, wet soil and green growing things tinged with the sweetness of decay and humus.

My father hadn't exaggerated when he said it would take one man all summer. The garden was alive as I was, but not a single plant had a bud on it, rose or otherwise, and the box hedges leaned more towards hedge than box. Even the flagstone path was hard to distinguish in places where the weeds choked it. As though it had truly not been touched in a hundred years.

But—everything was green. Vines snaked over walls,

clambered over archways and doors. Hooked canes sought my sleeve at every pass. Dead wood showed up everywhere I looked for it, but it was largely invisible beneath the pulse of life that ran over everything. Like an electric current flowing along the outer shell of a conductor.

The first flecks of rain grazed my arms. I didn't want to get caught in a downpour. My sense of direction led me east towards the edge of the garden, where the garden house stood. I couldn't see it from inside the garden itself, though the gables of the main residence were just visible over the tops of the tallest hedges. I picked up my pace as the first real raindrops fell, and I failed to heed the warning flagging of my left foot.

I tripped. I stumbled a few steps over the path, a clumsy, childish movement, until at last I managed to arrest my own momentum by grabbing at a plant. My right palm exploded in pain. I had caught hold of the rose bush nearest me, and it dug vindictive thorns into the soft pad of my flesh. I cursed and let go. The offending cane swayed in release, more snake than plant, and I pulled tines out of my skin. Unease curled in my gut. I found my balance again cautiously. I tested the foot, flexing back and forth, and was relieved that I seemed to have regained control.

I had prevented my father from coming on the basis that he might not be able to handle such a large task, but what if I could not? I didn't have the advantage of my father's magic. The garden might have defeated my father's stamina. But it might destroy me. I wiped my bloodied and shaking hand on my jeans. I walked, one cautious step and then another. Gaining confidence, gaining momentum. I breathed easier.

In front of me stood a small clipped-gable bungalow with eaves that hung heavy with the thick-thorned briars that grew up the walls. It was much simpler in style than the main residence and at least a few decades younger. Where the main house had beckoned, this one turned in on itself, quilted in its nettled layer of protection. I had the sense of a house asleep, dreaming through the decades.

Yet from the chimney came that gentle stream of smoke.

Fat raindrops bruised my shoulders as I clambered up the stone steps and knocked at the door. A voice responded, deadened by layers of wood and vine, little more than an affirmative hum and possibly a figment of my imagination and the growing sound of rain. But it was enough to go on.

The door opened directly into a front room that seemed to take up most of the downstairs. The floor was covered in a thick rug, pinned down with a coffee table and several upholstered chairs. A staircase and a door nestled together at one end, but the rest of the walls were obscured by shelves and shelves of books. Someone had installed what looked like easy-build bookcases on every spare inch of wall, with books of every color, shape, and size.

The effect was overwhelming. Not that of a neat and tidy library, but of someone's study, a collection gone long under-curated. A set of antique faded volumes near my shoulder stood next to modern copies with shiny dust jackets. Books lay sideways on top of other books, crammed into the shelves such that no spare inch of space was wasted. Looseleaf pages and slim notebooks spilled out at the margins.

The whole thing tilted towards a tiled fireplace opposite the staircase, like a copse of trees gentling down a hillside.

A fire pulsed in the hearth, lighting up the spines of the books like the flicker of an old movie. A wing-backed armchair was pulled up close to the light, its shadows deep and hidden. It took my eyes another moment of adjustment to reconfigure the shadows into the shape of a man, slunk into the chair like a cat. He had a book on his lap spread open to the light of the flames.

"Hello," I said.

He reared back like a garden snake. "Who are you?"

I took another step forward and stopped, my empty hands held out. "My name is Ethan Keating Mendoza."

"Keating."

He couldn't have been much older than me, maybe thirty. He was a repulsive person, hair greasy and unkempt and nearly colorless in the firelight. His features, though regular and fine, were pinched and watery in his pale, gaunt face.

"Arthur Keating sent you," he said.

"Yes. I'm his son and business partner. I'm here to take the rosarian job." I felt too tall, like a looming giant, a threat, and for a moment, the man looked at me with a wide-eyed gaze that seemed remarkably like fear. What did he have to fear from me?

"He mentioned a son. I assumed you were a child."

"No," I said, spreading my arms as though to indicate my full-grown size. His gaze traveled over me warily. I let my arms hang back down. "But I've worked with my father on our home farm since I was a kid. He taught me everything he knows. If it's a Keating rosarian you want, I'm more than qualified." It was a memorized little speech, intended to sound professional and earnest. It came out petulant and unsure.

His lips twisted unpleasantly. "Did you inherit any of his abilities?"

My scalp prickled. My father hadn't mentioned telling this man that he was a hedge witch. Could a man who coaxed a bloom from a garden this long gone simply be nothing else? But. Abilities could mean more than one thing.

I cleared my throat and lowered my pitch. "I'm more than competent."

His eyes narrowed. "If you have no magic, then you are not suited to the job and I have no use for you. At least not alone. Return with your father and I will reconsider." He looked back down at his book. I was dismissed.

No.

"He's sick," I said quickly. I moved directly into his line of sight, so he that couldn't ignore me. "He can't manage a garden of this size, so it's me or no one."

He blinked up at me, astonishment spreading across his pinched features like molten wax. "And you'll tell me how to manage the estate, will you?"

"That's not what I'm trying to do."

"I'm perfectly capable of hiring my own people."

"I realize that. That isn't what—"

"Isn't it?" He shut his book and rose to his feet in a fluid motion that only emphasized his resemblance to a garden snake. Standing, he was taller than me. He had a slender, sinewy build. His hair fell well past his shoulders, and with the fire behind him, his face was in shadow. "You presume to take over for your father as gardener. Perhaps you think you would make a better trustee as well?"

He radiated hostility, eyes narrowed and jaw set. I instinctively retreated from anyone so angry, and yet—he had meant to give a rose to a child. "A garden in this state will take an immense amount of work. I can handle the physical labor better than my father can. You need a rosarian." I spread my hands. "I'm here. And more than capable."

His eyes hesitated over my hands, and I remembered too late the blood smeared across my palm. But the look on his face changed, his lips softly parted, as though in thought. "Make it bloom," he said.

"What?"

"You said your father taught you everything. So do what he did. Make it bloom."

I clenched my hands, and the pricks from the rose bush burned. "I can't make a rose bloom on command."

He turned back to the fire, and the angles of his face in profile looked hollowed out, a stone angel in a dying garden. "You can wait out the weather. Then go home."

"But—"

"Please," he said softly. "Just get out."

THREE

RAIN GAVE WAY to pellet-sized hail as I ran back for the main house, as if determined to add literal injury to insult. Hail, in June. The weather was apocalyptic.

Inside the butler's pantry, I shook the ice from my hair like a dog. The cold lunch had been swapped out for a meal more suited to the weather, hot pies and steaming soups. "You must not have heard," I said. "I've been fired."

The house, of course, did not respond except perhaps to make the food steam more appetizingly. I was too angry to eat, my stomach roiling in acid frustration. He hadn't even given me a chance. Sure, I wasn't his original choice, but this place needed *someone*. It was a wreck, overgrown and choked with weeds and not healthy enough to bloom. Abandoned but alive, improbably and stubbornly alive. All it wanted was care, and I could be the one to give it.

The silence quivered.

I forced down a pie, my bitter consolation prize. It was delicious, which made everything worse. I liked this house. It was lonely—and so was I. Perhaps we could have found solace in one another.

Slowly the hail ceased pounding outside, leaving nothing but the soft hiss of rain on the flagstones. It was time for me to go.

As I turned away, a glint from the dumbwaiter caught my eye. A watering can sat on the tray inside, a wine bottle sticking up out of the mouth. Next to the watering can were the pruners and gardening gloves. I picked up the gloves. They were beautiful, made of thick oiled leather. Useful if the garden felt like caning me again.

I put down the gloves and pulled out the wine bottle. The label was faded and in French. One line in particular needed no translation. I nearly laughed aloud. *Vin rosé.*

"Wine for roses?" I looked around as though Colonel Mustard might be right over my shoulder. "I was fired," I said again. "Your guardian doesn't want me here." I squeezed my right hand. The ache felt sharp and hooked, as if the thorns still lingered in the skin.

I opened the back door and stared out at the gardens. The long trellised archway, overrun with vines, protected the flagstones from the worst of the rain. Even from the doorway, I could see how overgrown the roses were. How the long canes, desperate for sunlight, had grown upwards and outwards without agenda. They waved at me through the mist.

I could do it, I thought. If I wanted to. If he allowed me. I could do it.

Prove it, said the Colonel over my shoulder.

I pulled the gloves on.

The stone flagging led like a maze to cozy, private corners. Each one featured a centerpiece rose or two, occasionally grown up and over a trellis. I could identify the more obvious ones, the mosses and albas distinctive enough to stand out even amongst the madness. Others offered no end of possibility. I could not have concretely identified most without a bloom. Every single cane ended without a bud at the end—blind shoots, they're called.

The main path down the length of the garden was lined with tall standards, large rose trees that had long since been overrun, like the rest of the estate, with red-burnished Virginia creeper and other vines. My father had never kept rose trees—they were a lot of effort for someone who made a living selling cut roses, and in the Midwest they often needed to be uprooted and wintered on their side to survive the winter. The effect could be gorgeous, though. Especially a proper rambler in full bloom, tumbling down from the top like a woman's hair. I pulled the creeper from the standards as I went, dropping the vines on the ground.

By the time I found the garden folly I was properly soaked. Built at one end of the reflecting pool, it looked like the ruins of a Greek temple in miniature. Convenient, since the "ruined" roof would allow plenty of sunlight for the rose that was trained up and over the archway situated above a marble bench. This was the Madame my father had encountered. The one that had bloomed. Rain streamed down the entirely-green plant. Whatever magic my father's presence had wrought was long gone. The Madame was just like every other plant in the overgrown garden.

Just behind the bench stood a statue of a woman, a seashell beneath her feet. Aphrodite, the goddess of love, with Virginia creeper wrapped around her shoulders. She watched me warily, waiting to see if I would do something other than drip onto the floor of her temple.

"The first step, Madame," I said. "Is to prune."

Cutting back once-blooming plants, which I had to assume most of these were, in the middle of the growing season might mean losing the chance of a bloom. But they couldn't go on as they were. I wandered aimlessly, assessing, pruning back plants only where they were in my way. My right palm burned when I squeezed the pruners. I took care to stay clear of the garden house.

Along the western edge, I came across a wall made of stone rather than box hedge. It was tall—taller than I was—and I couldn't see inside. I estimated the room was no more than fifteen feet square. An incongruously small space that would, by effect of the high stone walls, lay in shadow most of the day. It didn't make sense for roses, which need full sun.

Perhaps it was a tool shed. I doubted the original owners would have wanted dirty gardeners traipsing through the main house, getting dirt on the carpets and making the guests uncomfortable. So the garden designer had included a tool shed within the gardens themselves. Like the garden house, which had probably been meant as a place for the hired help to stay, outside the main residence.

Curious, I followed the wall around a corner until I encountered a wooden door. The door was relatively free of vines and overgrowth. As though it were still regularly used. I knelt to examine the plant at the base, a climbing rose clearly intended to grow up and over the head jamb. It had been cut off, brutally low to the ground, perhaps as recently as spring. It had sent out a new cane, which dangled across the barred entry. It was red-green, the color new foliage sometimes takes, and soft and mossy to the touch. I pulled it gently out of the way.

A lock on the door was long since broken, the latch hanging loose. I grasped the handle with a deep sense of unease that took me by surprise. *It's just a tool shed*, I told myself. A tool shed, not a crypt.

The door swung quite easily. As though last opened quite recently.

It wasn't a tool shed.

It was a small, open-air garden room like the others. Grasses and sharp thistle covered the ground. When I looked closely, I could make out the perimeters of old garden beds. It had probably been a shade garden—those had been popular with the Victorians—but most of the plants were long gone.

Except one. At the very center of the garden room, in the place that would make the most of the limited sunshine, grew a twisted, ugly rose bush. It stood a good five feet tall, with malformed foliage that sprouted from canes with a horrifying number of thorns. The leaves were spindly, deformed witches brooms instead of rounded leaflets, a purple-red froth that reached with a death's gasp towards the sky.

Rose rosette disease was one of the few diseases that had no cure. It was fatal, always. It produced horrifyingly deformed plants, and worst of all, it could spread. The best course of action for a rose with RRD was to dig it up and burn it.

The adrenaline twisted its way through my nervous system, sharp and hot, and the hair on my arms stood up. The plant was a living corpse, decaying and contorted and *wrong*. It had clearly been sick for a long time, and only its isolation had kept it from infecting the rest of the garden thus far. But eventually, it would.

I closed the door behind me and didn't look back. I had wasted enough daylight, gray as it was.

I hiked out to the front and grabbed my loppers from my truck. Then I started on the perimeter, hacking the rose beds down to about two feet or so. The rain eased as I worked, then picked up, then eased again. I fell into a rhythm with nothing but the slicing sound of my loppers and the green rattle of the canes as I threw them in a heap. I would need to locate a wheelbarrow and someplace to burn them. I had a feeling the house would provide.

The last bush hissed when I tried to cut it. I pulled the loppers back. Enchanted estate or not, a sentient rose bush seemed beyond the pale.

Then it meowed, and a small creature emerged.

"Oh," I said. "It was you."

She was a small black cat and stared at me reproachfully with yellow eyes as suspicious as Aphrodite. No doubt I had destroyed her favorite hiding place.

"I'm sorry," I said. "I won't need to cut everything down to the ground, just the perimeter." I hoped that was true. If I cut everything down to sticks the bushes would spend all their energy on regrowth and none would be left for blooms.

The cat licked a forepaw and used it to rub down her

face, which had gotten a bit ruffled up by the sharp canes during her escape.

"Don't get careless." I decided it was no less ridiculous to talk to a cat than to a butler's pantry. "You could lose an eye. I knew a barn cat who tore an ear once."

She raised her tail high and stalked off—and then stopped and turned, gazing at me over her shoulder as though to make sure I would come along.

I followed her to the edge of the property where the rail fence marked the boundary. One of the ancient oaks stood sentry, and I stepped beneath the canopy. The cat slipped under the lowest beam with a soft mew and was gone, thin tail disappearing between the corn stalks that pressed up right against the fence, already almost as tall as my knees. I wondered if whoever owned the farm knew their property backed up against an enchanted estate. If they ever thought about who owned it or what in the world it was doing there.

The rain eased to a soft mist. I took out my phone and turned it on. It registered a single bar of service. I fired off a text to my father, letting him know that I was okay and that cell service on the property was spotty. Then I switched it off again. If I couldn't convince the man in the garden house to let me take the job, I would be going home tonight anyway. I could explain my failure then.

As I put the phone away the breeze picked up, swaying the corn. Despite being wet I was warm from my work, and I propped my elbows on the fence and leaned into the wind gratefully. Ahead of me, between the corn rows, I saw movement—a person. A woman.

She moved like a mermaid through an ocean of green

corn, her fingertips trailing along the tops of the leaves. She was barefoot and wore cargo pants and a tank top, her long dark hair pulled into a ponytail through the back of a baseball cap. I stilled as she approached. I had never seen a hedge witch work like this before, but I assumed that was what she must be. A hedge witch hired by the farm to help the corn along. She approached the end of the row, and she turned her head and saw me. She was very pretty, with brown freckles across her nose and younger than I had first thought, perhaps just out of high school. She grinned at me from underneath the bill of her baseball cap. Then she turned and walked back up the next row, still brushing her fingertips over the corn, her toes leaving soft impressions in the wet dirt.

LIKE THE REST of the garden, the briars that climbed the walls of the garden house had been allowed to run wild a long time. The tips were green and ran off the edges, waving in the breeze. Those still attached to the stone sides of the house had mostly died off, ropes of brown thorns wrapping the little house like chains.

I hesitated on the stoop and tugged at the ends of my shirt, double checking I hadn't missed a button. I had swapped out my shirt for a dry one, but I couldn't hide my wet hair or shoes. Hard work, my father said, always paid off. If you gave even the smallest of responsibilities your full attention, then more opportunities would come your way. A man who could be trusted in small things would be trusted with greater ones.

My mother's mouth would always twist when he said that, and when I grew older I understood why. Hard work paid dividends in the form of golden opportunities for some people, usually those who had more resources in the first place. The rest of us had to work twice as hard for the same outcomes. For us, hard work just meant more hard work. And in the end of course, it wasn't true for my father either.

My mother had emphasized the importance of maintaining a presentable appearance to the outside world. When you couldn't look the part, you could at least dress for it. At this I tended to fail miserably, which growing up I first attributed to my being a boy. Then to being a farm kid. Until I was finally forced to acknowledge that my reluctance was a product of my own unique, stubborn temperament.

And so I knew that I had spent all day pruning and weeding for almost certainly nothing. I would be fired again at best, accused of trespassing at worst. All while looking like a ragamuffin.

I knocked at the door. A black whisper slipped between my feet.

The black cat meowed and twisted herself once again through my legs, a sleek black figure eight. I bent down to scratch her between the ears.

The door opened.

"What are you doing here?"

I looked up to find the man—the trustee—staring at me as though I were something that crept through a crack in the baseboards. His hair had been combed back from his face, and it looked more yellow than it had by the firelight, like the color of straw.

I straightened up. "I've been working in the gardens," I said cheerfully. "I'm here to update you on my progress."

"You were fired." He shook his head. "You were never hired to begin with. I told you to leave."

"I can't leave."

"Can't?" His eyes widened, frightened. "What do you mean, you can't?"

I inhaled and felt the gardens, the house, and everything within it, stop to listen. "Can I come in?"

His eyes were wild, darting everywhere, looking over my shoulder into the garden as though for some lurking threat. Perhaps that was why he stood back to allow me into the house.

"I've been out in the gardens all afternoon, taking a closer look. I pruned some of the outer hedges—that took most of my time—and made a plan for how to approach the rest of the garden. I'd like to focus on pruning the largest roses first, since in many cases they're restricting sunlight to the other plants. This would be a rough cut, for speed. We can worry about the shaping after."

He sat down at the edge of the hearth and looked up at me, his elbows on his knees. "You mean you won't leave," he said.

"The garden wants me here. The house wants me here. It's like it knows *why* I'm here. It gave me wine for the roses."

"Wine. For roses."

"It was a rosé," I said. "Get it? Rose wine. It gave me gardening gloves too, and a watering can, and a set of tools."

"Wine for roses," he said again. His eyes were still wide, but his gaze settled on my person, wandering from my damp hair to my wet boots on his carpet. "I would not have thought of that."

The garden caught its breath and held it, and it was like the silence before something momentous, the moment when Caesar held his thumb aloft.

"Look," I said as soothingly as I could. "The rose, the one my father took. You told him to give it to me. It lasted all week. The bloom—it was already fully open, it shouldn't have had that long of a vase life. But it did. It was beautiful."

His features shifted as I spoke, eyes narrowing and mouth hardening. He looked shrewd. "You said you had no magic."

I had seen my father's magic, lived with it, knew what it looked like and how the roses responded. A rose lasting all week was at best an act of preservation, not of creation. But it was what I had, and I laid it at his feet, a guilty feeling curling in my stomach. A willingness to work hard I had in abundance. But I was promising something that I might not be able to replicate, even if it were useful.

I swallowed down the guilt and shrugged. "I can try."

The look hardened on his face. "If you can get anything to bloom, I will double the fee promised."

My mouth opened. I shut it.

He dug in the pocket of his jacket, a loose-hanging thing in a threadbare velvet, and withdrew an ornate skeleton key hung from a red tassel. "There's a wine cellar off the kitchens, if you need more for the roses."

"You aren't—I don't know—saving it for something? Don't people do special things with old wines?"

"The owners have been dead a long time. And technically you work for the estate, not for me. It seems reasonable that you make use of estate resources." He stretched up to hand me the key, and I closed my fingers around it. The metal was warm. "Directives. Don't uproot any roses. Kill nothing. And avoid going into the garden when it rains."

I shifted in my sopping shoes. "Why?"

He hesitated, but then frowned and said, "For liability purposes. And be careful. Wear your gloves."

"I've worked with roses before," I said, laughing. "I promise I know they're thorny."

The cat meowed, annoyed at being ignored, and twisted herself around the man's ankles. He pet her. So she was his cat. It figured. Who else could she belong to?

"I'll want a report every few days," he said without looking up. "And if anything looks like it will bloom, let me know at once."

My blood bubbled with excitement. "I'd be happy to show you what I've done, if you'd like to inspect."

"I don't go into the garden," he said shortly.

"At all?" I was surprised, though that certainly explained the man's pallor. How did one *live inside a garden* and never visit it?

"I don't like to leave the bungalow if I can help it."

"Why?"

"Plants die when they're uprooted."

"Not always," I countered. "Sometimes isolating a plant can allow it to recover in more controlled conditions." I thought of the plant with rosette I had discovered that afternoon, which no amount of isolation would fix.

"Perhaps I am a convalescent plant, then."

"You're not a plant. A plant would be out in the sunlight, not hidden away inside." I remembered belatedly that I wanted this man to trust me. "I meant—"

"I don't care much for roses," he said softly. "Their blooms are beautiful, but the rest of the year they're nothing but a briar bush. And these haven't flowered in years."

"Then why do you want them to bloom so badly?"

His expression was sour, and he chewed his lip for several moments before he answered. "My mother was fond of roses," he said at last.

"So was mine. She admired the way they protect themselves. They don't let themselves be used easily."

He looked me over slowly, as though really seeing me for the first time. "Aren't we a pair," he said softly. "I haven't my mother's talent for gardening and you haven't your father's agreeable nature."

"I got shoved around a lot in school," I said easily. "I don't let it happen anymore."

"No, I don't suppose you do. Perhaps tenacity is a virtue in gardening." His eyes alighted on my hands. "You're injured."

"What? Oh."

He stood up and I held out the injured hand. I hadn't bothered to cover it, and the largest puncture wounds were an ugly purple.

"A cane got me, but it looks worse than it is." That was a lie. Thorn punctures hurt like hell and the imaginary barbs left in the skin lingered for days. But I had also taken thorns to the face over my career. So, not the worst injury I'd ever sustained.

"May I?"

I nodded, and he opened my calloused palm with fingers so thin the knuckles stood out like flower bulbs. He had soft skin, the kind of hands people have when they spend most of their time indoors. I thought of one of the boys I had liked during that year at IU. A computer science major with the softest fingertips I'd ever felt.

The pain in my hand suddenly flared. I felt each pin prick acutely—three. How had I not realized there were exactly three? I gasped, and the pain was gone. A trio of pink pinpricks shone faintly in the firelight, a triple stigmata. But the wounds and pain had resolved.

I looked up in astonishment. "You're a witch."

"Not the useful sort," he said. Before I could ask what might be more useful than healing wounds, he sank slowly into the armchair, his head in one hand. He had gone somehow even paler, and he slunk into the wingback chair like a mole retreating into its burrow.

"Are you alright?"

"Ask the house for better gloves," he said into his hand. He didn't look at me.

"I wasn't wearing gloves at the time."

"Then do." He took a deep breath, and it sounded labored. When he looked up, his colorless eyes were urgent. "You don't want any more injuries from this garden."

FOUR

THE NEXT MORNING I woke to rain still pelting the balcony doors.

I glanced at my watch. Nearly 9am. The lack of sun had failed to wake me, and I felt the prickling of the caffeine withdrawal headache that came with oversleeping. I rolled over and caught sight of a small breakfast laid out on a silver tray on the nightstand.

Yesterday with all of its hard work and strange men in little briar-covered houses came rushing back to the forefront of my consciousness. I had been hired after all. I let that small triumph nestle into my chest, warm and satisfying. Then I swung my legs over the side of the bed and reached for my breakfast.

It didn't have the look of Colonel Mustard about it. Corn cakes with jam and peanut butter and a steaming pot of tea, accompanied by a small crock of honey. The arrangement said, quite clearly, that this was a perfectly acceptable breakfast for someone who intended to laze about in bed all day. Even if it was, technically, the weekend.

"Thank you," I said, just in case whatever or whoever had delivered the food was still listening, and I took the tray out to the covered balcony. The honey shone a deep gold in the gray sunlight. I dipped my little finger and tasted. The flavor was rich and evoked summer plants. I mixed a heaping teaspoon into my teacup. It helped a little with the headache.

As I ate, I let my eyes wander over the gardens, which looked like a watercolor map in the rain. The overgrowth wasn't as visible, and the various foot paths appeared relatively wide spread. I could just make out the walled-off garden room with the sick rose.

The trustee had said to keep out of the garden in the rain. The rain hadn't bothered me yesterday, but I was very conscious of the fact that I had wormed my way into a job through a combination of insinuation and trespassing. I wasn't about to go breaking any more rules than necessary.

I wandered downstairs with the thought of exploring the library. I had intended to study English literature in college and was hopeful a few old editions of classic favorites might be on offer, or maybe even one or two of the salacious novels the Victorians were notorious for. The library had dark-wood walls with Tiffany-esque stained glass windows of flowers and vines that let in a minimum of daylight. Presumably to preserve the integrity of the books. Wall scones at helpful intervals provided enough light to read the gilded titles. A few stuffy volumes of fiction by long-dead authors I had never heard of, but mostly business almanacs and reference manuals and ancient legal texts. Not a single book on gardening.

The stained glass windows stretched down to the floor between shelves of books and arched at the top like doorways. They depicted gardens, or pieces of one—lilies of the valley, roses growing up an arch. The rose window had a latch cleverly hidden along the black metal bars that held the glass panels in configuration. It was locked, an old-fashioned plate set cleverly into the metal frame. I thought of the skeleton key in my pocket. Perhaps it fitted multiple locks in the main house?

I pulled it out and inserted it into the plate. The lock turned, and the window swung in with it. I hesitated. I had just resolved not to go breaking any more rules—but the man in the garden house had said nothing about avoiding secret rooms off the library.

I turned sideways to fit through the slim opening and stepped into a greenhouse. It was a small space, about half the size of the kitchen, and empty save for a few old pots lined up along a workbench and a corner with what looked like more furniture covered in a drop cloth. The rain beat down on the glass overhead, and the noise soaked through the space like water through damp earth. I wondered what sorts of plants the owners had grown. The proximity to the library suggested it had been a space for specialty exotic plants, orchids and ferns and whatever else the Victorians had been into. A greenhouse with a more prosaic purpose, such as an all-year herb garden, surely would have been located nearer the kitchen.

A rustle from behind made me jump, but it was only the cat.

"How did you get in here?"

She looked at me and cocked her head, obviously flummoxed as to why anyone would doubt her ability to be anywhere she wished to be. She must have followed me in, silent on her delicate feet.

She jumped up onto the work bench and began a game of bat-around with a spare piece of twine, pulling it about the work surface. I wondered again at the lack of dust. Did someone come in to clean? And if so, why not throw away a spare bit of twine? It was as though whoever had last used the space had simply left and the accumulation of years never arrived.

The cat swiped the twine onto the floor and stretched, tail in the air. "Yes, well done," I said. "You've cleared the table."

She licked a paw and leapt lightly down. Ignoring the twine, she twisted off towards the other wall where the larger items were covered in drop cloths, including one that stood nearly as tall as I did. Probably another mirror. I frowned at it, irrationally annoyed at the Victorians and their insistence on checking their own excessiveness in every room in the house. Even the greenhouse wasn't safe. I supposed I should be grateful that the garden had been spared, save for the reflecting pool that had long since lost its capacity for reflection.

I pulled the drop cloth from the first pile, which turned out to be a stack of chairs and old tools, which I picked through, looking for anything that might be useful. Most everything was rusted or broken. Junk. The greenhouse had been used the way my father and I used the garage. Not for its intended purpose, but to store extraneous bits of everything.

I next lifted the edge of the drop cloth that covered the mirror-sized object, revealing the corner of what looked like a heavy frame. Intrigued, I pulled it off and found myself looking into the eyes of a man who gazed out of the frame with wide blue eyes. A young man, younger than me—maybe just twenty. He was golden-haired, thin but elegant, and tall, judging by the wild-eyed horse next to which he stood and to whose reins he held tight, as though only the strength of his gloved fist kept the beast from galloping into battle. I doubted very much the Victorians had stood around looking epic with horses, even the very rich ones. I peered closer and realized that in addition to the horse's reins he held an emerald rosary wrapped around the fingers of his other hand, crucifix dangling from his fist. Well, that was Catholics for you. Working class until we weren't, and then we very much weren't. The frame too was gilded and excessive, at least four inches wide and carved with a swirl of florals and tiny cupids.

Despite the absurdity of the man's pose, and the incredible vanity of having a life-sized portrait in one's own home—I had to assume this was one of the original residents—there remained something compelling about the portrait. About the man. It wasn't just that he carried all the self-possession of a person born into wealth and privilege, though he certainly did that. He looked at the viewer—he looked at me—as though he had a thousand questions. As though he would never stop peeling back layers until my soul was laid bare. Taken apart like clockwork to study and understand.

A tiny name plate at the bottom read: Aloysius Kilbride 1914. Not a Victorian after all—he was an Edwardian gentleman. He could not then have been the original owner of the estate.

He was almost hard to look at. Early in my adolescence I'd noticed I found it difficult to look at beautiful people. I had known I was gay since middle school, when my curious thoughts were all about the other boys. It wasn't until high school that I had realized imagining sex was difficult. As a child, I had imagined romance as something warm and soft, a pillow to cuddle down into. But as an adult, I'd found nothing but real people with sweat and body hair and chapped lips.

I hated that I reacted like I did, hated that my instinct was to curl in on myself. I wondered how many men I had confused, thinking they must have accidentally hit on a straight guy who they had been so sure was gay. I wanted to explain—that I liked men, that I might even like him. But the idea of a come on still made me want to crawl alone into my bed. I had to be coaxed out.

I frowned at the portrait, and the man gazed steadily back. I felt uncomfortably warm, the collar of my shirt pressed too close. My fingertips were sticky with honey. "You don't know me," I said. The only response was the rain beating on the glass roof.

All at once the cat streaked from the room like her tail was on fire. She pushed at the glass door with her forehead and slipped back into the library. I followed her and found her waiting by the front door of the residence, sitting and staring like a dog waiting for its owner. I heard the unmistakable sound of wheels rolling up the gravel drive and threw open the door.

A blue pickup rolled up and parked behind mine, and a

woman climbed out of the cab. She held a brown grocery bag, and her head was bent against the rain, but she smiled and waved when she saw me.

"Hello," she called. She looked about fifty and had a freckled, windburned face. Her hair was the color of sun-bleached hay. "You must be the new gardener," she said. "Suzy Landress, well met and all. Would you mind grabbing the other bag? There's one more in the cab." She pointed towards the blue truck in the drive.

I brought in the other bag and helped her unload in the kitchen. A small mountain grew on the countertop. Bread and cheeses and flour and vegetables, most of it raw and unpackaged, the kind of supplies you'd find in a farmers market, not a Kroger.

"I didn't know anyone else worked here," I said. I was absurdly pleased to have another person to talk to. Colonel Mustard and the cat were decent companions, but they couldn't talk back.

"Oh, I just deliver groceries once a week," Suzy said. Her voice was cheerful and clear with a gentle Midwestern tang. "I'm here every Saturday. Who d'you think brings in all the food for that poor boy?"

I shrugged, not wanting to admit all my suspicions about an enchanted estate to a complete stranger. "I'm Ethan Keating Mendoza."

"Keating Mendoza," she repeated, and stopped unpacking long enough to squint at me. "Your mom is Spanish?"

"Mexican," I said, automatically stiffening, but she only nodded.

"I live up the road. Which of course here means a few miles and half a dozen cornfields."

"Are you a farmer too?"

"Me? No." She shook her head. "I keep bees. Bring honey to farmers markets and crunchy grocery stores."

A beekeeper. Of course. "It was your honey at breakfast!"

"Oh, did you like it?"

"It's fantastic, especially on corn cakes."

She smiled, and her face cracked open like dirt under a hot sun. "That's what I bring to the farmers markets, to let folks dip in a honey sample. Nothing as good as honey and butter on fresh cornbread."

She began putting groceries away. The vegetables went into baskets and the cheeses into the old-fashioned ice box. She'd even brought a freezer brick for the top shelf, to keep the produce beneath fresh.

"Can I help you?" I moved forward to lift a yellow summer squash, but she waved me off.

"I know where everything goes, it's faster if I do it myself. Besides, you're on break, aren't you?"

"I—well. It's been raining all day."

"It does that here. Something about an air pocket or—I don't know, I'm not a meteorologist." She laughed. "It's always been funny in this area."

"Here? You don't mean just at the estate?"

She shrugged. "Sure seems that way. Not that there's much else for a few miles in either direction. Takes some monitoring when you're working outdoors. I'm sure it will be sunny tomorrow. I certainly hope so."

"Do you garden?"

"What me? No, just bees. Not a gardening bone in my body, though lord knows my grandmothers tried. I've killed cacti, succulents, all the sorts of things that are supposed to survive even when they're not particularly well-cared for. I'm a teacher. High school. My students think it's funny, bringing me a cactus and watching it dry out in a classroom windowsill. I teach history. American, but only because I've been waiting for the World History teacher to retire or die. Man's been teaching for fifty years—literally fifty years, still thinks the USSR is on the other side of the Iron Curtain."

I laughed. I liked people who were willing to talk without expecting me to be extroverted or clever. Suzy seemed happy to chat without my input.

"I love old houses like this," she went on. "There's a surprising number in Indiana, leftover evidence of the Victorian oil boom, most of them. I always take my AP Seniors on a field trip to one in the spring."

"Do you ever take them here?" I asked.

She shook her head. "Private property. Louis wouldn't want strangers traipsing around the grounds in any case. I'm sure you've noticed how he is."

Louis. So that was his name. It was so normal, so unassuming. I thought of the man in the garden house, reading in front of the fire, and wondered how on earth to describe him. "He seems very private."

"It's more than that. He won't leave the estate. I'm not sure he'll even leave the garden house at this point. I've wondered if I should tell him to see a doctor or... but it's none of my business." She shook her head again and put the last of the potatoes into a wooden box on the countertop and turned to face me.

"Can I get you something to drink?" I hesitated, looking around. Thanks to the Colonel I didn't even know how to get myself a glass of water, let alone serve a guest. But a pitcher of water and two glasses had appeared on the marble top behind me.

"Oh, that's very kind, thanks," she said as I handed her a glass. If she noticed the sudden appearance of the serving ware, she didn't say anything.

"So no one else ever comes here? It's really just us?"

Suzy leaned against the marble top opposite. "Well, the place is supposed to be cursed."

I choked on my water.

She shrugged again. "Just local legends, from at least the time when I was a kid. The place looks abandoned, which doesn't help, but it never really was. There was always a trust, and the trust contracts with some of the locals, for groceries and repairs, that sort of thing. Henry Kilbride sold off most of the land before he died in 1917, and he put the house and grounds in a trust, along with whatever was left of the inheritance. There always has to be a trustee, whose job it is to hire those of us who look after the place. That's Louis. And I'm the only one he's contracted with right now. Well, and now you, of course."

I'd heard of trust fund babies of course, but beyond the largely-fictional conception I'd derived from novels, I knew very little about trusts. I'd never considered the possibility of a trust that just existed, sans baby, on and on. "The Kilbride family?"

"The original owners. Old Catholic political family—like the Kennedys, but—oh, I suppose you're too young for that reference."

I laughed again. "I know who JFK was."

She waved a hand. "Yes, but not just him, it was the

whole *family*, they were an *institution*. I try to tell my students, but they just never quite get it, I think. There's never been anything quite like them. Probably for the best, we're not supposed to have royalty. Anyway, the Kilbrides were sort of like that, but of course back in the day they couldn't hack it with the WASPs on the east coast, so they came out here, where they could still pretend they were better than everyone else. The matriarch was Elizabeth Kilbride. She had a grand vision of a rose garden, that's the only thing she really wanted. Her husband made a lot of money investing in land during the oil boom, and she was young and beautiful and he wanted to give her anything she wanted. So he bought a bunch of property here—they used to own everything for miles around, that was before it was farmland of course—and she built herself an English rose garden."

"Was she English?"

"Maybe by blood. But if she was, she married down, what with the whole fraternization with a Catholic Irishman. But she had so much rose magic she supposedly maintained it all by herself. The Kilbrides hosted politicians and oil barons, even foreign dignitaries. And everyone always said the rose garden was the finest they'd ever seen."

"It's a lot of work for one person," I said lightly.

"So much work that she started hearing voices, said the roses were talking to her. She was packed off to an asylum, and she died within a year. The official record is that she starved herself to death, but abuse was common in those places in those days, so that strikes me as unlikely. Hard to starve yourself such that no one notices. In any case, the gardener was gone, and Kilbride himself died after a few years—he was an old man by then. There was a son, but he was disinherited and the historical record drops off there. So the property was empty, and a third party hired to act as trustee to look after roses that know they've been abandoned."

"And that makes it cursed?"

She raised her eyebrows. "A rose garden that runs wild, but never blooms, and never dies? A man holed up in a garden house, cut off from the world?" She smiled suddenly. "But you're here now, and I'm sure you'll be able to set it to rights. I've been telling Louis to hire a proper hedge witch for years."

My stomach twisted. "I'm not actually a hedge witch," I said.

She squinted at me over the top of her glass. "You sure about that?"

"I've worked with roses all my life. I think I'd know by now if I had an affinity for them. I'm just an average rosarian."

"Well, I didn't say you had to have plant magic. I never noticed anything special about the way bees behaved around me until I was forty." She looked at me intently, as though she expected me to confide that, now that I thought about it, I *had* noticed odd things happening around me in the garden.

I shrugged helplessly.

"Well," she said, in a brisker tone. "Average rosarian or not, I'm glad Louis has finally come around. He must've seen something special in you. Welcome to the Kilbride Estate."

I walked her back to the front, and she promised to see me again next week with more groceries. I wasn't to worry about food until then, since she provided for the estate and that meant everyone *on* the estate. I thanked her politely and watched her drive off, tires crunching on the wet gravel, and I thought about curses and asylums and the sound of rain on a glass roof.

JUNE MELTED INTO July. Every day the antique thermostat on the kitchen porch climbed above ninety, and every few afternoons, black-bottomed thunderheads rolled through. The roses loved it. They grew like the wild things they were, even the ones that had been cut to the ground, sending new growth up in search of the sun. Once I finished trimming the perimeter, I moved on to the box hedges, hacking them down into a rectangular shape, and finally onto the largest centerpiece roses, which would take the most care.

Every night those first few weeks I went to bed flat with exhaustion. I had been gardening all my life, but my body wasn't used to such brutal hours, and my joints and muscles ached by the end of each day. When I finally climbed into bed, I was asleep even as my head was still sinking into the down.

In the mornings I always stopped by the butler's pantry for my breakfast and water bottle, which the Colonel always left filled for me along with the watering can and a new bottle of wine. It wasn't always a rosé—sometimes it was a white or red. The colors of roses. I had taken to diluting the wine with a little water and spraying the roses with the mixture. Some people used vinegar as an organic spray. I figured the wine might work the same way.

I ignored the walled room with the sick rose. With the door shut and the rose isolated, its chances of spreading were—well, still not zero. But thinking about it made me feel sick. The door tugged at me ominously when I passed it, and so I began to avoid that too. The way I ignored when my foot flagged and made it hard to walk. I would deal with it. Eventually.

A few times a week, I updated Louis on the garden progress, though I had little to talk about beyond the ongoing pruning. He was stiff and formal, glancing obviously at my hands and person, as though to make sure I had suffered no more rose injuries. It was unfortunate, I thought, that we couldn't have developed an easier relationship. It would have been nice to have someone to talk to between Suzy's weekly visits and the daily texts I sent to my father by the edge of the property. Someone who could have been a friend.

My hair grew long, curling around my ears just enough to be obnoxious in the sticky heat but not long enough to tie back. The second Saturday in July, Suzy showed up with a barber kit in tow. There was no point, she said, in my wandering around looking like I had no one to take care of me. She cut her wife's hair on a regular basis, and this meant I was in excellent hands.

She sat me down in the lowest chair we could find, and as she spread a towel over my back, her hands surprisingly gentle, I realized I had not been touched in weeks. Aside from the cat and the roses, I'd had no physical contact with another living thing since Louis had held my hand to heal it. A bit of contact that he seemed to regret.

"Your ears are chapped." Suzy misted my hair with a spray bottle. "You'll want to put Vaseline on them."

The tops of my ears had sunburned, and then peeled, and then burned again.

"I'll ask the house," I said, my head bent over as she trimmed the curls that fell over the back of my neck. The *snip-snip* of her scissors made my skin prickle.

"Ask the *house*?" She finished trimming the bottom and brushed the hair off the towel with her hand. Brown curls tumbled to the floor.

I grimaced. Suzy seemed to accept the fact that the house maintained itself completely unaided. But we never discussed the presence of Colonel Mustard. "Don't you... talk to it?"

She paused, her hands still on my shoulders. "No," she said finally. "Should I?"

"It makes meals for me. Turns the lights on."

She resumed lifting segments of my hair, snipping the ends. "Oh, well, yes. Louis is a powerful magician. He's got quite the system set up here. And he's very bookish, you know. Like my smartest students. I've always told him that if he wanted to go back to school, that'd be a great option."

A *magician* was a more generalized—and powerful— practitioner of magic. Someone who studied theory in school, who understood how to manipulate the forces that governed the world. They existed mostly in academia, as far as I knew. Hedge witches, like Suzy and my father, had specific talents, usually related to something in the natural world. They were common in agriculture and family-run enterprises.

The magic Louis had performed when he healed my

thorn wounds seemed like hedge witch magic. The sort of thing that was useful if you worked in a garden or if you took care of people or animals. The house's magic couldn't be Louis'. Louis never came to the house—at least, not in the weeks I had lived there.

And besides, the house didn't feel like him. Colonel Mustard was a personality unto itself. The Colonel was how this house was *supposed* to feel. When I was little, our family home had given the feeling of a family dog. Welcoming us when we arrived home, sitting at our feet while we ate dinner together or watched television. After my mother died, the spark that lived in our house had gone dark and sad.

I'd forgotten about that until coming to the Kilbride Estate. I'd left it behind, along with other childish things. But it had been very real to me once. Perhaps that was why this house seemed so friendly. Why I knew I was safe. The gardens were wild and possibly dangerous, a place I loved but had to fight with every day. But the house existed for my comfort. It needed nothing from me. It wanted only company.

"All set," Suzy announced and swept away the towel. "You might want a shower to take care of the little hairs."

I walked her out. At her truck, she hesitated. "You do check in on Louis, don't you? I don't mean to sound like a mother hen, but I do worry."

"I—speak with him. Occasionally. About the progress in the garden."

She nodded, though she looked unhappy, and I felt unaccountably guilty. Surely if Louis would rather be left alone then it was better to let him be?

Suzy sighed. "For a while, he talked about bringing another hedge witch in. I offered to place an ad for him, interview candidates, but he hated the idea of having that many people traipsing through."

I remembered suddenly. "There's a hedge witch who works next door. I saw her helping the corn."

Her eyes lit up. "You've met Harmony?"

"I—no, we only crossed paths. You know her?"

"My niece. My wife's niece, by blood. She's a wonderful girl, a rising senior at the school where I teach. She took a summer job next door. If you see her again, tell her you're Suzy's friend."

FIVE

I WATCHED SUZY drive away with a sinking feeling I recognized as loneliness. Colonel Mustard was a wonderful companion, and the cat had a habit of turning up right when she was most wanted. Suzy had called me her friend, but she came only once a week. The rest of the week, I had no one to talk to.

After she left I showered and dressed for dinner. I had become accustomed to eating all my meals in the butler's pantry or in my room. An elegant place had been readied for me every night of my first week, and I had studiously ignored it. After that, a little bistro table and chair had appeared in front of the sideboard. On drier evenings, the bistro table relocated itself out onto the porch, and I lingered over my meal as I watched the first fireflies dance up out of the grass. By dusk the top of the garden house was but an outline in the darkness, a single window glowing faintly orange over the gloomy garden wall.

That evening, I arrived at the porch to discover that my usual table was missing despite the pleasant evening. My stomach growled petulantly, and I ducked inside, hoping that dinner hadn't been canceled altogether. My appetite was stronger than it had ever been at home.

The dumbwaiter in the butler's pantry was piled with its customary array of too many offerings, though it was all packed up in little paper boxes like a to-go order at a nice restaurant. Next to the boxes was a bottle of wine. The house had only ever left me wine in the mornings, which of course was for the roses. This time, it had left two wine glasses as well.

And—a picnic basket. A large, old-fashioned wicker affair with a flap at either end and secured with a leather belt. I packed up the paper to-go boxes, which fit like a perfect Tetris solution, with the wine glasses on top.

Had I wished aloud for a friend, or had the house read my mind? Or was it not me who the house was looking out for after all, but Louis? If I had any doubt the house's magic was not from Louis, this certainly settled it. The man in the garden house would never have deliberately sought out my company. Yet I was so lonely, I was apparently willing to seek out his.

It was a beautiful evening, cooler than expected after the heat of the day. The kind of evening that crops up once or twice a summer and makes you start to dream of fall. It was still warm enough for fireflies, who began to flash at my feet as I made my way through the early twilight towards the garden house. At the front door, I nearly lost my nerve and turned back. As I hesitated on the stoop the door suddenly opened, and Louis appeared in the bug-spotted twilight.

"Keating?"

His face was flushed, splotches of dark pink dotting his cheekbones in uneven patches. He wore a heavy wool peacoat, though I was perfectly comfortable in a flannel button-down, and his hair was somewhat better trimmed than before, falling in an even sheet to his collarbone. I wondered if Suzy had visited him too.

"Keating Mendoza," I corrected. I held up the heavy basket. "I brought dinner. The house always leaves way too much food for one person. Colonel Mustard seems to think I'm underfed."

He blinked. "Colonel Mustard?"

"I may have named the house."

He nodded as if this made all the sense in the world and stood back to allow me inside. I deposited the basket on the table, and Louis shed his coat and crouched down to stoke up the fire.

"Were you going somewhere?" I asked.

He hesitated, just the briefest pause in the motion of the thin wrist that held the poker. "No," he said. "No, I have nowhere I need to be."

I held up the bottle. "Do you drink wine?"

He stood up and brushed off his hands. "I did once. What is it?"

"I don't know," I admitted, peering down at the label, which like most of the others was written in French. It didn't have a varietal or regional name that I recognized. "But Colonel Mustard has excellent taste, at least in food. So I imagine it's just as good."

"Have you been using it? The wine?"

I told him about spraying the foliage while I worked the corkscrew. "Some people use vinegar as an organic pesticide. I suppose the wine is doing the same thing." The cork came with a *pop*.

He hummed. "I should think it more likely that the wine is a kind of stimulant."

"A stimulant," I repeated. I'd never heard of such a thing for a plant.

He walked to the bookshelf that stood directly to the right of the fireplace and pulled down a heavy-looking hardback that might have dated from the turn of the last century. He flipped carefully through the ancient pages. "Here's Bellinger on the subject. 'As regards vitality, plants and animals differ in several ways, firstly in mobility...' so on and so forth... no, here it is, listen: 'The plant, having roots, is a creature of ruthless uptake, enlisting all substance, whether freely given or sought out like a succubus, for its own life force.'"

He looked up at me with an expression that strongly suggested this ought to have meant something to me. I cleared my throat. "And so what does the... life force have to do with the wine?"

"It isn't the wine per se. Bellinger means magic when he says vitality, it's just an old fashioned way of looking at it. It's the way they talked about magic when this was published. There was still a rather classist prejudice towards hedge witches in general. But he's saying that plants absorb anything and everything. They have roots to take in water and nutrients, leaves to collect sunlight. Even pollination is a largely passive process, from the plant's perspective. Of course today we know this isn't altogether true; plants can influence their environment in any number of ways. But compared to mankind, to the animal kingdom, it remains largely valid. Plants absorb, because that's the only way a plant has to be. And so that must be the way they relate to magic as well."

He had an odd way of speaking—an accent I couldn't place, and he spoke like he was still quoting from the old book. "So when a hedge witch shapes plants…"

"The plants absorb whatever they can from him. Blood, sweat, tears. There's a transference of vitality."

"I don't think—"

"I don't mean it quite so literally. For example, your father's attention to the roses could be considered a kind of sustenance. When he turns the full power of his focus on the plants, they take it. They take whatever they can from it."

"So those of us without magic just can't give the right kind of attention?"

He frowned. "That's the bit I don't think science has ever really explained. Theorists are clear that for real transference to occur, there must be some kind of intention. But stronger and more *intentional* transfer is of course much more difficult to enact. And inversely, a hedge witch with a particular affinity, such as your father for his roses, might be able to impart influence with comparatively little effort at all. Magical affinity enables a kind of subtlety."

This all sounded very academic, bordering on nonsensical. But then, I had never studied magical theory. I had avoided the subject altogether once I realized I wasn't a hedge witch. "And if you don't have any capacity for magic?

What's the opposite of subtlety?"

"Sacrifice," he said simply. "And wine is a sacrificial in many religions. I've never heard of it being used in this context, and I do find it strange that none of the theorists I've read have ever mentioned it, but..." He seemed to realize then that he was still standing as though orating from the book, and he lowered it.

"Well," I said. "If wine is good for roses, perhaps it's good for you too."

He took the glass I offered. The dark liquid glinted like rubies in the firelight. He closed his eyes as he inhaled, lips parted, and took an awkward, halting sip. As though he had never drunk from stemmed glassware. A deep red drop clung to his upper lip.

"Are you hungry? I'm not sure what's in here." I had no idea what to expect in a Colonel Mustard picnic. I folded back the paper boxes and produced several varieties of hard cheeses; three kinds of savory pies, one of which smelled as though it might be a curry; a caesar salad; and a lemon poppy seed pound cake. I spread them out on the coffee table. At the bottom was a half-bottle of a dessert wine I didn't remember seeing before.

"This I can read," I said. The label was thoroughly modern, a 2016 vintage. The liquid inside was honey-colored and glowed in the firelight. I supposed Suzy must have bought it. When I glanced up, Louis was watching me, a little nauseated-looking. But he continued to drink as we ate, and the wine worsened the flush across his cheeks. The food and wine disappeared, and I refilled both glasses when they emptied.

The second glass went down even easier than the first,

and when we had eaten most of the food, I opened the dessert bottle, which was so sweet it made my mouth pucker. The black cat jumped up into my lap where I sat on the sofa, eliciting a stare from her human so jealous that I laughed.

Louis had grown more languid with the wine, melting into the armchair cushions. "You're a traitor, Telegraph," he said mildly.

"Telegraph." She rubbed her cheeks against the buttons of my shirt. "That's an interesting name for a cat."

"I'm sure she has her own name," he said. He yawned, fighting the same wine-induced slumber battle I was currently facing myself. "She's like a messenger. She brings me things—trash from neighboring farms, scraps of newspaper. A source of information about the outside world."

"She's good company." She sniffed interestedly at my wine glass, and I dipped a finger into the golden liquid and held it out for her to lick. She licked with a sandpapery tongue, then shook her head and jumped from my lap in offense. I laughed again.

Louis watched her run off into a dark corner. "I don't—" He cleared his throat. "I don't entertain much these days. I have nothing to offer a guest."

I looked pointedly at the little feast, which we hadn't quite managed to finish. "What else could we want?"

He shrugged again, that same strangely languid movement that managed to convey casual disinterest even as it made him seem vulnerable. "I don't know. Cigarettes, or an after-dinner brandy. Playing cards. Don't gentlemen usually keep those sorts of things?"

"I wouldn't know. My father only drinks beer, and I only

ever had the cheap kind of wine in college. You know, whatever the freshmen can get their hands on, which is whatever's cheapest or the upperclassmen don't want. Usually comes in a box." I mimed pouring a glass from a plastic pressure spout. "It was always bad. But one of our buyers at a grocery store gave us a nice bottle as a gift last year, and we opened it on New Year's. I liked it. Not as much as this, though." I filled his glass with the dessert wine. It was sweet, and I loved it. Louis smiled tentatively at me, a cautious bird hopping towards me, one step at a time. The hope fluttered in my chest, and I wondered how to make him do it again.

"You were a student?"

"Briefly," I said. "I dropped out of school to take care of my father when he got sick."

He cleared his throat. "Is he well?"

"Yeah. He's doing alright. I text him every day. There's a little bit of cell service on the edge of the property." I hesitated, feeling the question at the edge of my lips with the wine. "Suzy mentioned you had wanted to hire hedge witches, once. There's a girl who works the corn on the bordering farm. If you were looking for someone else. Suzy's niece."

"A child."

"Nearly an adult, according to Suzy. If you needed someone to maintain the place, next summer—"

"No." His voice was quiet, polite, and final. "Thank you."

The silence that followed was heavy, laden with my unstated admission that I had no magic, that whatever he had imagined he saw in me was at best an illusion and at worst a lie. I floundered. We had been so close to something approaching easy conversation.

"Do you know," he said after a few moments, "I think I've read every book on these shelves. Suzy brings me new ones, from time to time, and I read those too. But I won't ever know everything. And that thought terrifies me."

His voice was surprisingly sturdy for a slender person who'd had three glasses of wine in rapid succession. But no one ever sounded completely sober waxing poetic about books.

"There's a library in the house," I said, grateful for the turn in subject. "But it's very dry."

He smiled. "I suspect I've already stolen anything interesting. You're welcome to pursue my collection, if you like. Though I think it's mostly medicine and magic."

He was no more handsome when he smiled than when he scowled, but he was so strange, so delicate, I felt it like a hook in my chest. Like a thorn through a glove.

He occupied my thoughts all the way back to the house, a prickle vine I couldn't dislodge. But I thought I understood. He was like a rose. It reminded me of the bouquets my father made for the grocery stores. First he stripped the thorns with a knife, making the stems smooth and harmless. It made for a more palatable bouquet, suitable for the average consumer, but it shortened the vase life of the flowers. If you were going to survive being cut from your source and trapped in glass, you needed a few thorns to survive.

THE ROSETTE-DISEASED plant had to go. I would put it off no longer.

But my spade, when I went out to my truck bed, was gone. I figured the house had put it somewhere, but a thorough search of the premises turned up nothing, and my attempts to ask the house were met with silence and a conspicuous lack of shovels. The house had never acted except to help me. I didn't know why it would steal from me, much less take an instrument I intended to use to protect the garden. So I wasn't yet afraid, but I was frustrated and confused.

My brief, pleasant interaction with Louis was not repeated, and my loneliness doubled down. On Saturday I seized upon Suzy like a drowning man thrown a life raft. Her straightforwardly kind, thoroughly Midwestern presence felt like pulling up a quilt on a rainy day. She brought extra honey because, she said, I loved it so much.

"Can I pay you for these?" I asked when she handed me what had to be five pounds of honey in an odd assortment of mason jars and recycled squeeze bears.

"Oh goodness, no," she said with a firm shake of her head. "At least not with money."

"How then?"

"Tell me about your garden."

It wasn't my garden, but I didn't argue. I told her about the new shoots and growth, the Madame that grew like a romantic shelter over the marble lovers bench in the Temple of Aphrodite. I talked about culling the worst of the dead vines from the garden house. I'd had to cut them all the way to the ground, and I told her about how they would regrow, soft and beautiful, and frost the house like a cake.

I talked more than I ever had in Suzy's presence. "Sorry," I said, embarrassed. "You probably didn't need that level of detail."

She chuckled. "It's normal. You're in love."

"I'm sorry?" I paused with my hand on a cantaloupe.

"You're in love. With the garden. It hasn't had anyone to care for it in so long, it's no wonder it's responded so well to you. How could it not, when it finally has a proper person to look after it? The soulless estate trust certainly doesn't give a damn."

I thought of the soul in the garden house who cared enough that he was willing to hire a rosarian but not enough to inspect the gardens himself. I diverted my thoughts like a stone thrown into a stream. "Actually, I think the Supreme Court has ruled that trusts are people too."

She chucked a turnip at me. "Smart ass."

I caught the vegetable and laughed. "By the way. Do you have a shovel I could borrow?" It seemed like a reasonable thing for a beekeeper to have.

She paused in her putting-away, a hand on the walnut cabinetry. "A shovel?"

"A spade. I didn't bring one. I thought the house might have one, but no luck." It was easier to lie than to claim that I suspected the house of stealing my shovel for mysterious reasons.

"I don't, I'm sorry. Why?"

She looked so suspicious that I laughed again. "I promise I'm not going to murder anyone. I'm a gardener. It's a perfectly reasonable accessory."

She swatted the air near my shoulder. "I meant, what do

you want it for? I thought you were just pruning?"

I told her about the garden room I had found and the rose sick with rosette.

The line between her eyes deepened. "But why does it have to come out? Can't a disease be managed?"

I shook my head. "It's contagious. It could kill every rose in the garden."

"I don't mean to tell you how to do your job. I just—well—I know that Louis won't be happy if anything is uprooted."

"I'll speak to him first," I agreed. Surely, Louis would be more rational than his various caretakers about the damned plant.

She sighed. "Louis can be—well, you know."

"I know," I said quickly. "I know."

MY FATHER HAD taken a cutting from the Madame with the intention to propagate it. That was what rose rustlers did, albeit usually with permission—take a stem and attempt to create a new specimen of the same variety. That's what a rose variety *was*. Genetically identical plants, most often grafted onto an established rootstock. Rose breeders carefully cultivated varieties to develop the newest roses with the most enchanting blooms, the best disease-resistant leaves, and propagation was how those varieties were reproduced. The old roses were so spectacular because they had survived the generations, still-beloved, not-forgotten, by gardeners who for generations had done exactly as my father had—taken cuttings and hoped, with a little water and care and magic, that they might strike. That was what my father had been hoping to discover for so long. A little piece of beauty he could reintroduce to the world.

I took three cuttings. Three seemed like a safe number, a magic number. Propagation often failed, but if I could get even one of my cuttings to strike, it would still be a success. I could take them home, if Louis didn't object. We didn't have a Madame at home, and even though it was hardly the long-lost rose my father had been searching for, it would look lovely in our garden. I would train it up and over our back porch door, a place where it wouldn't be a part of the commercial garden. It wasn't the Temple of Aphrodite, but it would do.

I took my cuttings to the greenhouse, which would make a nice home for the delicate new plants. The stems I had taken had no flowers or buds of course, so they needed no additional trimming. I laid them out in a row on the potting bench in the greenhouse and lit a match to sterilize the knife. Then I slit each stem vertically along both axes, dividing the bottom bit into quarters. Normally, a rosarian would use a rooting hormone to encourage the stem to put out new roots. But because I didn't have any, I dissolved some of Suzy's honey in water and dipped the split stems in the honey-water.

Three of the discarded ceramic pots did nicely for holding my baby roses. I set them up in a neat line along the south wall and filled each with a mix of soil and compost. Finally, each stem went into the dirt in its own pot, and I watered them well.

"Grow," I told them.

I swept the work surface clean. I felt calmer in the greenhouse. Inside, even the sounds of birds and insects fell away, leaving only the green-tinged silence. The greenhouse might not have had any plants besides my cuttings, but it was a place dedicated to living things. A place where I knew what I was doing, with no one to judge me.

Except, of course, for the portrait of the handsome young man. He looked out at me from his gilded frame, as though wondering what I was doing back in his domain. His beauty was other-worldly. The artist must have improvised. It seemed likely a commissioned work would seek to portray its patron in the most flattering light possible.

"Imposter," I accused.

He looked back at me impassively.

I threw the dust cover back over him.

SIX

I LAY AWAKE in bed that night long after the time I ought to have been asleep. It was a cool and breezy night, and I had left the French doors propped open with a few of the heavier legal tomes from the library. A book on estate law rested on my knees, a volume I had selected from the library out of sheer boredom.

The lights in the house were attuned to my habits, and the lamps began to dim just as my eyes began to burn and the words on the page began to slip from their lines, swimming like minnows darting in a stream. I fell into the hazy world of half-dreams, my tired brain returning to the endless pruning of the garden, rehearsing the mixing of the water and the wine, until I came up for air, gasping.

It took me a moment to work out that I had been awakened by a noise. The sort of sound I would not have given a second thought to at home. A car door shutting or a storm door slamming. Simple evidence of life, proof that I was not alone.

I sat up and the book I had been reading slid from the bedcovers to the floor, landing with a thump that sent a jolt running through my blood a second time. The lamps in the room had come back on to a soft glow, and I could see my watch. Just after midnight.

I went out onto the balcony. The wind had picked up in the night, and I hugged my arms around my bare chest. There was no indication of what might have made the sound that woke me. It was dark, and the lights from the garden house were out. I could hear no vehicles, nor animals, nor thunder. Perhaps I had dreamed it after all. The cold was bracing, good for chasing off the grogginess-induced anxiety, and I felt my equilibrium return. And with it, no particular desire to go back to bed. I wondered if Colonel Mustard would prepare an herbal tea and honey if I went wandering downstairs in the middle of the night.

The first raindrops came lightly, like a mist, but thickened quickly, washing away the last vestiges of the dream. I was about to turn away from the balustrade when from the direction of the garden house I saw a tiny pinpoint of light, dim in the falling rain. I peered through the mist. The light bobbed its way along the path that led from the garden house to the reflecting pool. A flashlight. I leaned over the balustrade, tracking the light as Louis moved through the gardens, until finally he must have gone around a box hedge, and the light disappeared.

I threw on a shirt and my sneakers and hurried down. I found a black umbrella in the butler's pantry, and I took it with me. The labyrinth of the gardens was dark, but it was my labyrinth, and I knew it by the sound of my footsteps on the path, the length of my pace. Wherever Louis had gone, I could no longer see his flashlight. I scanned the tops of the box hedges, searching for the glow, and nearly tripped over something in my path.

Telegraph meowed up at me piteously.

"Sorry, girl," I whispered. "What are you doing out here? Shouldn't you be asleep?" She blinked at me with eyes that shone through the dark. Her fur was damp. Didn't cats hate water? "Do you know where Louis is, girl? Where is your person, hm?"

She blinked again and turned away, heading down the path, and I followed. The rain beat down on the umbrella, a loud thrumming that made it impossible to listen for movement. Telegraph slipped through the rain like she was born to it, her pace utterly unbothered. Finally the glow of the flashlight peaked over a yew line. Telegraph turned sharply and headed towards the western edge of the garden, towards the light. I followed, and when we reached the walled garden, she sat down at the entrance.

The door stood open.

In the center of the garden was a bright light, and in front of the light was Louis. He had set the flashlight atop a satchel or backpack, the light angled towards the sick plant, next to which he knelt in the dirt. He wore a bright white shirt, the sleeves rolled to his elbows, the black peacoat crumpled next to him on the ground. He reached a bare arm into the tangled plant and wrapped his fingers around the thorny canes, pulling them fiercely aside. He grunted in pain, a low, abject sound in the dark. With his free hand, he reached into the depths of the plant, digging for something I couldn't see.

I bit down on my lip, and my teeth were like thorns in my flesh. After a long minute, Louis withdrew his arm, unhooking the canes that grabbed onto his skin with their surplus of thorns. His arm shook, and his fist clenched tight around something small that he put into his chest pocket.

He sat silently for a few moments, breathing heavily. Then he cursed and began pulling tines from his skin, tossing them at the base of the plant.

I tasted blood and realized I had bitten through my lip. My face was wet, and I thought I was crying, but then realized that at some point I had dropped the umbrella. The rain ran down my face into my mouth, water mixing with the blood.

Louis moved to stand, and I fled.

MY LEGS BURNED. Everything looked terrifying in the dark, every plant might as well have had rosette, for the amount of thorns that tore at my shirt, my flesh, as I ran.

Was this why the house had stopped me from uprooting the sick plant? Why Suzy had tried to dissuade me? Because they knew Louis needed it for—what? If what I had just witnessed was some sort of magic, then it was unlike any I had ever seen. I had no idea what kind of twisted magic required a man to torture himself on a thorn bush in the dead of night. What kind of magic demanded its pound of flesh.

I stopped in front of the garden house, gasping and properly soaked. I leaned against one of the walls, bare from where I had cleared it of vines, and slid down the stone until I collapsed into the wet grass.

My heart pounded. I was a coward, but not so much of one that I could go back to bed, pull the downy covers up over my head and tell myself it had been a dream. It wasn't a dream. It was a nightmare, and I had to wake us both up.

The rain droned on. Wherever Louis was with his flashlight, I couldn't tell. The cold stone behind my back felt like ice through my shirt, and I shivered.

Was this somehow part of the curse that Suzy had insisted was only a legend? Was this why generations of townies had known to steer clear of the place, where men were driven mad by roses, and plants fed on wine and blood? Or was it simply another symptom of Louis' isolation, a compulsion to tear his own skin in the garden? Was there even a difference? I bent my head against the wet stone and closed my eyes.

I heard my name. A hand gripped my shoulder, slim but strong. Louis stood over me, the black umbrella held over both our heads.

"Get up," he said harshly and pulled on my arm.

He led me through the house to the little kitchen at the back. It was a small space, with barely enough room for a range and ice box around the small table set with two chairs.

There was a single head pendant hanging above the table. Louis pulled the chain and the bulb crackled into life. Then he took the whatever-it-was from his pocket and put it on the counter, then slipped off the peacoat and put it over the chair next to me. It smelled of wet wool.

I sat silently in my chair and shivered as Louis filled a kettle with water. After he had lit the range, he produced a dressing gown from a cupboard and threw it over my shoulders.

He must have known I had followed him to the walled garden—he had found the umbrella—but he didn't ask questions, just quietly took down two teacups when the kettle sang. I wasn't sure if I wanted an explanation or a confession, or if I even wanted him to speak at all. His long hair had been tied back, and it hung in a wet mass over one shoulder.

"I followed you," I said to his back. "I'm sorry I went out in the rain, but I saw your light and—I was worried. I saw what happened. With the sick rose."

"Ah," he said in a flat voice. He took the thing he'd placed on the counter and dropped it into one of the teacups. Then he pulled a teabag from a cabinet and placed it in the other. He poured hot water over both and brought them over, one in each hand.

The cup with the teabag he slid towards me, gently such that it didn't spill. I lifted it and let the steam wash over my face. It was warm and good and smelled distinctly of—

"Roses."

He smiled. A tight, thin smile with no humor in it. "From the last time the garden bloomed. Along with some other herbs. It will help you to forget. And to sleep."

"Forget?" I set the cup down, and a little of the hot liquid splashed onto my fingers. "I don't want to forget."

"But I want you to." In the stark light of the overhead bulb, he looked as insubstantial as ever. "And I'm afraid I have to ask you to play by my rules."

His exposed forearm glowed where it rested on the table. The sick plant had left vicious lacerations in his flesh. "First tell me why."

He looked away. I thought he wouldn't say anything, but then he sighed and said, "There was still a full staff when I became trustee. The staff kept the residence in order, and I kept the gardens. It was my responsibility." His fingers flexed on his cup, and I wondered what he had put in his. "One by one, they all left, and it was just me and the garden."

I shook my head. "That's impossible."

"How so?"

"Suzy told me about the local legends. The garden had run wild by the time she was a kid. She heard the stories. The estate had been abandoned for decades by then."

"It was never abandoned," he said sharply. "But yes, I'm sure she did."

"But you can't be more than thirty," I protested.

He looked from my face down to the cup of tea I held, still un-drunk. "I was named trustee shortly after Armistice Day."

"Armistice day," I repeated dumbly. "The armistice of... what?"

"The armistice in France," he said slowly, "in 1918. This bungalow was renovated the following March for the trustee, and I moved in to take over my responsibilities."

"But that was over a hundred years ago."

"The roses stopped blooming fifty years ago. Your father was the first hedge witch to enter the gardens in over a decade, and the very first rose magician. And only one rose bloomed, even for him. A single goddamn blossom."

He said the last words in a voice that was calm, steady. Resigned. A shudder ran through my body as I stared at him, trying to figure out if he was screwing with me. My lips moved several times before I managed to croak out, "And you? How are you... still here?"

He turned his palms up on the table. "It's like time has become unmoored, somehow, from this place. From me. You've noticed the weather behaves oddly? That's part of it. The world has forgotten this place, and so it uses its own rules. And the garden suffers for it. At first, every spring when the roses began to grow, I would beat them back, but every year the growth became harder to control, until finally the roses became nothing but growth, and they stopped blooming altogether." He looked down at his injured arm, his face even more wan than usual.

I followed his gaze and felt another shock of disgust. I believed him. It made a kind of twisted sense. Why the garden never died, why legends had grown up before Suzy's time. Why the roses didn't bloom.

"Are you trapped here?"

"I don't know," he said simply. "At first I went to the residence when necessary, and otherwise I kept to the garden. And then I left the garden less and less, and then after a while... I didn't."

I felt the inklings of panic at the edges of my awareness, softly whispering for my attention. "You told me to wear my gloves. You warned me not to get pricked."

He shook his head softly, the wet mass of his hair sliding over his collarbone. "I am bound to this place, not you."

That wasn't, quite, an answer. "So it is cursed."

"Of course it's cursed." He didn't speak for a moment,

and he looked down at the cup in front of me. It had stopped steaming. "Drink your tea. It's not wine, but I promise it's good."

I curled my hands around the cup but didn't lift it. "How much will it make me forget?"

"Only tonight." His voice was soft, gentle. Convincing. "A few hours. You'll go back to your own bed, and you'll wake in the morning well-rested. Nothing here can hurt you."

"Except for the garden," I said, but he shook his head again.

"I am the one entrusted with this place. You have nothing to fear."

"And what about you?" I asked. "I'm just supposed to forget that you're trapped here, and do battle with a fucking thorn bush to survive?"

"Yes. Because this is my responsibility, not yours."

I looked at him in disbelief. My hands were still curled around the warm teacup, and the heat traveled through my arms to my neck, like I was drawing anger up from the tea. "Not my responsibility? You hired me to heal your garden, to get the roses to bloom! And then you ask me to forget that you torture yourself for that same reason. Do you do this every night?"

"It isn't the same. You have been hired by the estate; and when your terms are completed, you will go home. My choices are nothing to do with you."

"Louis," I said, and waited until his eyes found mine. "Tell me what I can do."

His hands gripped his cup so hard the tendons popped against the skin, white and ropey. "Whatever ability you have to help the roses along the way, I would be very grateful. But this is not something you can change. Therefore." He inclined his chin at my teacup. "Drink."

I pushed it towards him, sloshing tea onto the table. "Fuck your potions."

I made it as far as the door before he said, "Ethan."

I turned and met his gaze. I expected him to say something. *Don't tell Suzy*, perhaps, or *Please forget this happened*, or even *Pack your bags and go*. But he said nothing, and after another moment, I turned back out into the pouring rain.

I DID NOT go back to sleep that night. Every time I shut my eyes I saw Louis in the walled garden, his soft hand wrapped around a thorn bush.

When the rain finally cleared in late morning, I went out into the garden. I followed the pull of my feet without question. Even as I walked, I dreaded it. Telegraph joined me, a silent, solemn shadow. I looked down at her, but her focus remained straight ahead, as though she understood the nature of our dark errand. When we reached the walled garden, she sat back on her haunches, tail twitching expectantly.

The sick rose looked no different that it had the first time I came upon it—a thorny mass. Telegraph trotted up to it and crouched beneath the lowest canes.

I knelt next to her in the damp dirt in approximately the same spot where Louis had the night before. The rain had washed away any evidence of blood, either on the plant or the ground. The rose didn't even look particularly disturbed.

I reached out a gloved hand and pushed it experimentally through the canes. The thorns snagged at the leather and it was difficult to push through, even knowing the thorns couldn't hurt me through the thick hide. Louis had to have nerves of steel to force himself to do it.

Deep inside the plant, I found what I was looking for. Some of the shoots had put out a few buds—of course this was the plant with buds—but they hadn't bloomed. Instead, where there should have been flowers, the buds burst into a mass of witches brooms, splayed out into twisted, aborted leaflets.

Vegetative buds appeared only on very sick roses. Louis had snapped a few of these off, which explained what he was collecting last night. I let the canes fall back into place.

The trustee, in the walled garden, with a thorn bush.

Telegraph mewed.

"You knew," I said. "That's why you were outside. That's why he told me to keep out of the garden in the rain." The rain gave him cover, and washed away the evidence. He hadn't wanted me to find out. And when I had, he tried to make me forget.

Did Suzy know too? The thought filled me with a rage that flared bright and hot and immediately faltered when I remembered my own cowardice, leaving a cold sadness at the pit of my stomach. How many caretakers had known that the trustee of the estate was suffering and simply did their duty and walked away? Could I do the same—finish the pruning, restore the garden, get a plant or two to bloom, and go home to my father?

"Maybe I really am a coward," I told the cat. "Or maybe—"

Maybe I could stay. Maybe there was something I could do, some way I could help. I knew nothing about curses. The house tried to help me but—

But it had taken my shovel. The house, which had foreseen my every need and provided gloves and pruners and a wheelbarrow, had hidden the one implement I surely needed to destroy the plant in the walled garden.

Eventually the RRD would spread. The disease was spread by mites that traveled on the air, they could infect rose bushes up to a mile away. And when that happened, the garden would die.

I closed the door behind me.

I wandered to the northern edge of the property, where I got a single bar of reception. It was the time of day I normally texted my father, but instead, I dialed his number, wanting to hear his voice. The call went to voicemail. I told myself it was a good sign—my father was out in the garden, pottering around much like I was doing. Not sitting in an ER room alone.

I got back to work and tried to focus on the weight of the pruners in my hand. But my chest was tight with anxiety, and I thought of bloody thorns every time a plant snagged my shirt. Telegraph nipped along at my heels, pausing every so often to play kitten with a dandelion or a blade of grass that had grown tall along the edges of the path. Perhaps she could sense my unease, could smell my worry about my father, who hadn't answered his phone and might have fallen—

No. I paused and looked around. I had worked my way into one of the smaller, more intimate corners of the garden, where the ramblers climbed over the walls, wild and free. When they bloomed, they'd be magnificent. If they bloomed. I knelt in the damp soil next to one of the more established ramblers. It was trained up against the wall, weaving itself along at about half my height. I reached through the tangled mass, gently stretching the canes apart, searching for the places where they were affixed to the wall. I located the first anchor around the thickest cane a few feet off the ground. It was firmly fixed in the mortar between the stones, but the anchor above it had come loose, which accounted for the sad droop of the plant.

I sat on my heels and craned my head back, charting the most elegant path up the wall. I may not have been a hedge witch, but I was a rosarian, and I could re-train a climber. That was craft, not magic. I added mortar anchors to my mental list of gardening implements to acquire.

I pushed myself back to standing, and the world turned upside down.

For a few nauseating moments, I floundered in the lack of gravity, no idea which way was up, sure that I would step off the earth and into the sky.

No, *no, no.*

I reached out, fighting to regain my balance, and realized dimly that I had caught hold of the climbing vines in front of me. I held on to them like a life raft and waited for the world to right itself.

Slowly, my inner ear course corrected, and the sky became the dome above me, the ground something to have faith in once again. I was on my knees, with one hand thrust into the rambler. I let go.

Thankfully, the elbow-length gloves had done their job,

and I was uninjured. I got to my feet slowly. Just a head rush, most likely. Momentary vertigo. I had barely been able to choke down any breakfast, upset as I had been this morning. My father's doctors were always warning that low blood sugar could aggravate the worst of his symptoms, since hunger could make anyone feel faint. I wondered if my father was bothering to eat right when I wasn't at home. I hoped he still made himself eggs for breakfast.

I made my way cautiously back to the main house, where I ate a full lunch and dinner, thanks to the Colonel. The vertigo did not return. I felt good, I decided. Steady in my body. Certainly well enough to drive. I had two more hours of daylight and it was only an hour's drive to my father's house. I could go home for a visit. The pruning was nearly done, and my roses would survive a few days without me. And I could swing by Home Depot on the way back and pick up the anchors—and a new shovel.

SEVEN

I THREW A few things—a few shirts, my only good pair of jeans—into my duffel and flew down the stairs. The first few raindrops hit my shoulders as I made my way out onto the drive. Large, heavy drops, the kind that meant the heavens were about to open up and unload themselves on whoever was unfortunate enough to be caught out beneath them.

I cursed. Why was it always raining on the estate? I jogged for the truck and threw myself into the cab just as the sky opened up. The rain pounded on the roof and hood with an unrelenting anger. It was like being parked beneath a waterfall.

I threw the duffel onto the passenger seat and lifted my ass out of the seat to dig the key from my pants. The jump ring caught on a thread in my pocket, and I was forced to snap it to free the key. Finally, I turned the key in the ignition. It clicked.

I frowned and turned the key a second time, but it continued to click. I cursed again.

I kicked the door open and threw up the hood under the pouring rain. I could handle basic car maintenance, but I could hardly jump a car without another engine to hand. Unless Louis was hiding a modern motor vehicle somewhere on the estate, I was shit out of luck.

Yet I continued to stand there, my head bent under the hood against the rain, staring at the useless innards of my truck. The rain soaked first through my button down, then my undershirt and jeans, until I was well and truly drenched, water running off the edges of my face. I was also, I noticed after a few minutes, shivering. The rain was cold.

The battery in my truck was less than a year old. We'd replaced it in spring, the last in a surge of large expenses. And I had been careful to run the truck once a week both to charge my cell phone and keep the battery in use. It shouldn't have died, not this soon. I pulled off a sopping shoe and used the heel to smack the battery terminals, then jumped back in the cab. My remaining sneaker made a squelching sound when I put my foot on the brake and turned the key in the ignition again. Nothing.

"Dammit!" I slapped my hand against the steering wheel. I shivered harder inside the truck, the way getting out of a cold pool is always worse than being in the water. I bent my head until my forehead hit the steering wheel and shut my eyes.

The garden wouldn't let me leave. I was stuck here until—what? Until I got the roses to bloom? Until the curse was broken?

The panic bubbled up so quickly all I could do was ride it as it seared through my veins. My mind screamed that my father was in trouble, that he was sitting in an emergency room somewhere in pain, and that I had no way of getting to him. Hot tendrils shot from my shoulders down my arms while I tried to remember how to breathe. I went from shivering to sweating in the space of a few seconds, and I kicked the driver door open again to invite the cold in.

I came back to myself in pieces. I was aware that I was cold again, but it felt like relief. I could hear the rain still falling, albeit more gently. Finally, I could make sense of the inside of the truck. The dash, the steering wheel, my white-knuckled grip. And a figure hovering over my left shoulder like a demonic angel.

"Keating," the figure said. "Keating, are you alright?"

Louis.

Louis stood in the downpour, one hand holding the black umbrella, the other pointing a flashlight at the ground. The collar of his wool peacoat was turned up against the rain. "Ethan," he said.

"It's cursed," I said to the steering wheel.

The flashlight jerked. "Well—yes."

"I mean, not just you." I swallowed against the fear that threatened to rise again. "It won't let me leave. The garden—my truck—" I started to shiver again, so violently my teeth chattered.

"You aren't cursed," he said firmly. He made a motion like he meant to grab my arm, then pulled back. "Come on, out of there. We need to get you warm."

"It won't start." I jerked my head at the dash.

"Probably just a dead battery. We'll get Suzy to jump it

next Saturday."

"But it wasn't—it shouldn't have died." It was suddenly urgent that I made him understand I was trapped, just like him.

We had to get out.

The garden wouldn't let us leave.

And it was killing Louis.

No. Louis wasn't dying. I wasn't sure where that thought had come from. It was the garden that was dying, not Louis.

He pushed the door open wider and put a hand to my elbow. That small touch shocked me back to myself. Balancing between him and the doorframe, I managed to climb out of the cab without collapsing. "The roses," I said. "They're going to freeze. All the new growth, it's going to die. The garden—you—everything's going to die."

"I'm a bit more worried about you at the moment, actually," he said bracingly. He had his arm around my waist. Once again, he was stronger than he appeared.

I leaned into the warmth. "It's fucking freezing."

"It's not, you're just wet. Let's get you upstairs and into the bath."

"I don't need to be *more* wet," I complained.

"It's the fastest way to get you warm. No heat in the residence," he reminded me.

"Let's go to yours, then. Fire's always on."

"Yours is closer."

"S'not mine," I said thickly. My mouth felt numb. "M'just the gardener."

He hoisted my arm farther up over his shoulder with a grunt. "Come on then, gardener."

He was taller than me, but not bigger, and we struggled up the gravel path together, me still with only one shoe. Thankfully the weakness in my left foot did not reappear. The stairs presented more of a challenge. Once out of the rain, my shivers turned to full-body-wracking shakes, like I had come down with a fever, and Louis had to support my right arm while I balanced against the stair rail with the left. Eventually we made it to my room where we found a small pile of firewood stacked in the fireplace near the hearth. Louis frowned at it. "Did Suzy bring firewood?"

"Must've been—Mustard." Though we were out of the wind and rain, he still had his arm around me, holding me up. Something was odd about that, but my sluggish brain refused to process what.

He pursed his lips, and I didn't have the energy to explain. He released me into an armchair—I spared a brief thought for the doomed embroidery—and bent over the hearth. I couldn't see what he did, but when he sat back a fire was already caught and going strong on the largest log. Like magic. I wanted to ask how he had done it, but my mouth had stopped accepting orders from my brain.

Louis went into the attached bath and turned on the taps over the tub, one delicate wrist cocked beneath the water to check the temperature. As usual the house had turned up the lamps, and his veins were visible in the harsh light. They moved beneath the surface of his skin like green worms.

When I fumbled the buttons on my shirt, he gently pushed my hands away and undid them one by one from top to bottom. He stripped the wet material from my shoulders and flung it on the floor. The Rob Roy pattern, dark with rainwater, stood out like blood against the marble tile.

I wouldn't let him help me with my jeans, and it took me at least five times as long as it should have to get them off before I could lower myself into the tub. The water was hot, prickling like thorns against my skin. I groaned as it settled into my bones. I wondered if it was painful to be a rose bush in the colder months, if they screamed as they shed their leaves for winter.

"The roses—" I started to rise out of the tub, a hand on either rim, but Louis shook his head.

"The roses will be fine. It's fifty degrees Fahrenheit. It's a cold snap, but it won't fall below freezing tonight." He had perched himself in the window nook, his back up against one of the window casings and his face turned toward the glass that went right down to the floor. It was dark outside, and the black glass reflected his face like a mirror.

I slid my hands back into the water. As I did, I noticed one spot felt more painful than the rest of my skin. I lifted the hand out again, trying to remember when I had pricked myself.

"You promised you would wear your gloves," Louis said softly. I met his eyes in the window. His reflection had a greenish pallor in the glass.

"I did," I said. I felt heat slide into my stomach, the beginnings of panic again. "I was. They must have been punctured. Is that—why I can't leave?"

"No." He spoke directly to my reflection, as though speaking face to face would have been indecent. "You're not cursed, you're only—sensitive. Sensitive to the roses, to their magic."

"I'm not. Sensitive to magic, that is. I told you that."

"Right," he said drily. He looked up towards the ceiling. "And I suppose that's why the house is so manifest to you. Remembers your favorite foods, brings you firewood when you're cold."

I shook my head, confused. "The house takes care of you too."

"It provides for my needs, yes. It's never struck me as a person before. Colonel Mustard, did you call it?"

"You could try thanking it from time to time."

"Idiot. You aren't cursed. Now relax before you give yourself another anxiety attack."

I sunk back into the tub and let my mind focus on the water, which was cradling and warm, no longer like thorns. The only sounds were the slosh of the water and the crackle of the fire in the outer room. Finally I dunked my head under and dragged my fingers roughly through my hair. It was getting long, and scrubbing it was painful. But it was a good pain, the kind that meant I was moving and doing, not the kind that meant I was slowly freezing to death.

I resurfaced and felt human again. "Thank you," I said.

"You're welcome." Louis glanced over his shoulder at me and then away again, his cheeks slightly pink. "I'm satisfied you won't pass out. If you're feeling better, I'll leave you to get some rest."

It finally occurred to me that I was naked, and in a bath, and that maybe I should have felt awkward about it. I didn't. "Wait."

He froze. "Are you alright?"

"Yes, I didn't mean—I'm fine." I swallowed. "Just not ready

to be alone."

He sank back into the window nook, his head against the wall. His hair fell back from his shoulders in a sheath, and his eyes were closed. The lines around his eyes squeezed into tight crow's feet. He looked like a portrait of a suffering saint.

"Tell me the truth," I said softly. "All of it. There are things you still aren't telling me, and I can't help you if I don't know."

The lines around his eyes continued to tighten, until his whole face was caught up in a grimace. "I was a medical student at Western Reserve. There were professors who studied this sort of thing at the University. Magic, vitality. The garden lives off me—off my time—somehow," he said to the ceiling. "I don't fully understand it. It's not completely impossible, according to what I've learned, but it's also not very probable, and there's no established case study to learn from. I came here immediately after I got the Order of the Boot from school. It took me about a decade to notice that time had stopped, that I wasn't growing any older, and another few years after that to realize I was deteriorating nevertheless. Becoming old without aging. Not properly dying, just losing vitality." He turned his head to look at me. "The garden should have died a long time ago. Roses don't live one hundred years, at least not like this, without anyone to care for them. But I'm tied to them, they're tied to me, and together we just sort of—go on. I'm sorry, I've never had to explain this to anyone but myself."

I grasped for what seemed like the most tangible thing. "You were kicked out of school?"

He looked down at his hands, which were curled in his

lap. "There was a professor. I did research for him, and I was—fascinated. First by his ideas, and then by him."

"You don't have to tell me anything you don't want to," I said.

He shrugged. "Not much to tell. We were found out. I took the fall, took the consequences from the school and my family. But it was his ideas, his theories, that inform what little I can guess about the garden."

"So the—technique—I witnessed," I said. "That's how the garden steals life from you?"

"No." His voice cracked, and he licked his lips. "That's how I steal it back."

"Jesus."

"Quite."

"How, though?"

He let his head fall back against the wall again. His eyes looked green in the low light. "It's a kind of symbiosis. It's easy to forget that plants are living things. But they're as alive as we are. They grow, they change, they reproduce, yes; but they also compete and cooperate and grieve. They need their own to survive, to thrive. There's documented evidence that plants are capable of learning, of storing memories. You've noticed that roses have a nasty habit of drawing blood from humans. Plants are particularly capacious reservoirs, known to harbor all sorts of metals and magics. Do you still use the wine?"

I nodded.

"Vintners used to grow roses at the end of their rows as a kind of bellwether. Roses attract pests and disease before grapevines do, which gives the winegrower a chance to get on top of a problem before it affects the vines. In a sense, wine owes its very existence to roses."

"Another symbiosis."

He nodded. "And anything that can conduct in one direction can do so in reverse. I can see how that might be exploited, turned into some kind of curse. When roses aren't given what they need, they can turn vindictive."

"So the wine is to placate them?"

He shrugged with one shoulder. "Perhaps. It makes as much sense as anything else."

"And you learned this from your…"

His lips twisted. "My ex-lover? Some of it came from him, some from the various hedge witches I hired over the years, some from whatever books I've been able to lay my hands on. The rest I've had to guess at over the years." He tucked his hands inside his coat, and I saw that his lips were the same greenish-blue as the veins in his wrists.

"Go warm up by the fire," I said. "I'll be alright getting out on my own."

When I came out of the bathroom the fire was still in full blaze, and Louis was fast asleep, curled up on the carpet in front of the fireplace like a cat. I pulled an extra blanket from my bed and threw it over him, then collapsed onto my mattress. It was barely eight o'clock, but I was so tired that my limbs felt like they were filled with something heavier than bones and muscle and blood, and I was asleep almost as soon as I could pull the covers up over my shoulders.

When I woke with the first light, the hearth held only my sneakers drying by the fire.

THE GARDENS WOKE up as I moved through them. Birds leapt ahead of me, announcing my presence to one another and flying away. When I made it to the garden house, I climbed the steps and knocked, then pushed the door open gently. The fire was out, but the clear windows meant the interior was well-lit. I could see the armchair into which was curled a deathly silent figure.

"Louis—Louis!" I shook his shoulder. His face twisted, and he made a half-hearted effort to shove me off. "Oh, thank god."

"Ethan?"

I fumbled for a lamp on the side table. Louis had one hand tucked between his face and the wing of the chair, and his eyes were still closed, though they were scrunched up in annoyance at the light. "Thank god," I said again. "I couldn't hear you breathing." I put a hand to his forehead, which felt warm. "I think you have a fever. I'll call Suzy, she can pick up some ibuprofen—"

"I'm not sick."

I sank to a squat beside him. His eyes were open, and the whites were bloodshot. "I'm pretty sure you are," I said slowly.

"Tired," he said, and shook his head.

"Here." I pulled a croissant I had shoved into my satchel after breakfast and pushed it into his hands. "Eat something."

I went to the kitchen for a glass of water. When I returned, Louis had taken a few bites of the smooshed croissant and was sitting a little straighter. I helped him take a sip of water.

"You look better," I said, and he glared at me.

"I don't need a mother."

I set the glass down on the side table next to the lamp. "You need someone."

He took another bite, resolutely avoiding eye contact.

"Has this happened before?" I pressed. "Does Suzy know?"

He swallowed a mouthful of water. "Christ, are you always such a woman?"

"Ass," I said, relieved. It annoyed my father too, when I fussed at him. In the end people liked to be taken care of. And that was what you did when you cared about someone.

He sighed. "No, Suzy doesn't know. Nothing like this has happened in a long time."

"So it's happened before? What does that mean?"

"Nothing. I told you, I'm only tired. Staying up all night to rescue hapless gardeners from the rain will do that to a person. Where were you going anyway?"

A diversion. I allowed it. "To visit my father. And to stop by a hardware store. I need a shovel."

"A shovel?" He pulled a hand over his face and squinted up at me. "What for?"

"The plant in the walled garden. It has rose rosette disease, it's fatal."

His frown deepened. "You want to dig it up."

"Yes, and burn it."

"No."

"It's deadly, it has to go. It will spread to the rest of the garden."

"I need that one."

"You can use another one, something that isn't sick. For

all we know that's what's causing this." I gestured towards his posture in the chair.

"I said no. It stays."

"But it's dying," I repeated pathetically.

He lifted one shoulder, unmoved.

I cast about for another angle. "It's recent, then? The rosette?"

"I suppose. Yes. But it had been years since I last visited the walled garden. A decade, maybe. I only began—trying again—very recently."

"A decade?" I said, stunned. "But you said…"

"It ought to be done more regularly, of course. I was advised to follow the cycle of the moon, although I suspect that was just an ancient practicality for people who didn't have regular access to calendars." His arm was uncovered and lay on the arm of the chair. There were still thorn pricks visible in his skin. "It's the only plant left in the garden with anything resembling buds."

My stomach pinched.

"Will you light a fire?" He had slumped back in the chair. Though he seemed a bit better after the bites of pastry, he was still folded in on himself, his lips deathly pale. "It's cold."

"No." I stood up. "We're going outside."

He frowned up at me. "I can't."

"I'm not talking about leaving the property, we'll stay in the garden. It isn't cold outside, and you need sunshine."

"I am not, as you've pointed out, a plant."

"And yet you're wilting." I held out a hand. "Let's go."

I closed my fingers around his and led him out the door. I had the sudden thought that he would follow me anywhere I asked. The sudden onslaught of sun blinded us both. He stood for several moments with his face buried in the crook of his elbow, hiding from the glaring midsummer sun.

"It's alright," I murmured. "I've got you."

I steered him by the arm into the gardens, coaxing and prodding until we were at the very center—the lovers bench in the Temple of Aphrodite, right beneath the Madame. In front of the bench, a little patch of grass and clover spread out in the full sun, and we lay down there in the sunlight.

It was warm, but not yet hot, and Louis kept his face turned up towards the sun like a flower. His eyes were closed, pale eyelashes trembling beneath the strength of the sun. In the light his eyelids were nearly translucent. Blue veins crisscrossed just beneath the thin surface, which undulated and fluttered with every inhalation. The muscles in his face began to relax one by one, beginning with the tightness of his jaw and spreading up his cheeks, releasing the strain surrounding his eyes, unfurling his brow.

I closed my eyes and let the sun warm my hair and face. "You said that you hadn't visited the walled garden in a decade before I came. Why not?"

He inhaled, exhaled. "I was tired."

"Tired."

"Tired of keeping the garden alive, tired of... everything."

"You mean you wanted to die."

"No. Maybe. I just thought that perhaps this was the natural end of things. Nothing is meant to live forever. The garden and I are proof of that. Eternal life corrupts."

I turned my head to him. "So you stopped trying to keep yourself alive. To keep the garden alive. But then you met my father, and he made a rose bloom, and you decided to try again?"

"No," he said softly. "Then I met you."

It ought to have been awful, to have him out among the plants that held him hostage in their strange, cursed symbiosis. But it wasn't. Peace melted into his face. The gardens were cursed, but they weren't terrible. It wasn't the totality of their essence any more than it was Louis'.

He really was like a plant, I thought. A rose bush. He was prickly, but all he really needed was some care and sunlight. Even the wine helped. I huffed.

"What is it?"

"Nothing, I just—I think the Colonel has a sense of humor."

"Why do you call the house Colonel Mustard?"

I laughed outright. It felt good to let all that stale air out beneath the sun. "It's a character from a board game. I used to play it with my dad as a kid. It was his favorite, so of course I decided it was my favorite too." I took in the scent of sun-warmed rose foliage, so like my childhood. "I wanted to be just like him. He was so strong. I used to think there was nothing he couldn't do. Before he got sick."

"May I ask your father's diagnosis?" he asked gently.

"MS," I said. "Multiple sclerosis. It affects the way he walks, sometimes. His vision and speech, too. He's been in remission for a few months now, but he had a bad fall a couple of years ago, hurt his hip. It made everything worse. That's when I decided to stay home. My mother died when I was in high school, and he needed my help to keep up the business.

We don't have an income without it. We negotiated a payment plan with the hospital but it's—a lot. And I couldn't be away from him, not when he might get hurt again."

Louis watched me from between blades of grass. A bee buzzed over us, seeking the clover, unbothered by our presence. We might as well have been two flowers. "I'm sorry. I'm familiar, a little. It's a difficult diagnosis."

I took a breath and let it out slowly between my teeth, then said to the sky, "I have it, too."

Beside me, Louis fell still. I told very few people, as few as necessary. My symptoms had only just begun last summer—a much more typical age of onset compared with my father—and I went into remission quickly. Quickly enough that most days, I was able to pretend it wasn't happening to me.

I couldn't look at Louis. "It's not supposed to be a heritable disease, but I guess my body didn't get the message. The doctor said something about how the genetic risk factors are elevated when you have a close relative with MS. That's the only thing I inherited from my father. I look like my mother, and I don't have an affinity for roses. I don't have any magic at all."

"I'm not sure I believe that. Look around us." Above our heads, the Madame waved green tendrils in the breeze.

When I looked back at him, he was watching me gently. "Do you need anything? Are you in pain?"

I shook my head. "My left foot flags sometimes. Foot drop, it's called. I don't feel it most days." Then there were the dizziness episodes, the occasional Jello legs. The things that hung like a cloud over the days when I otherwise felt fine.

"If there's anything I can do," he said. "Anything you need."

"Thank you."

I never talked about my diagnosis. My flare ups were less frequent than my father's and far less severe. Even so, I was used to downplaying my symptoms for my father, so that he didn't worry, and there was simply no one else to tell. The thought of going into detail with anyone other than a doctor was—not embarrassing, exactly. Alien. Intimate.

"You said that the curse knew that I was trying to leave. But it couldn't touch me. Could it be taking it out on you?"

He frowned. "It's possible. I hadn't thought about it like that. But... perhaps, if it had been accustomed to expending energy elsewhere, and then the object of that focus were removed..."

A rock sank in my stomach. "God Louis, we need to find a way to get you out of this."

"How? Break the curse?"

"Well—why not? A curse is a cycle, right? What did you call it, a symbiosis gone awry? So what if the relationship were corrected? No, listen," I said, as he squinted at me skeptically. "I know you're legally the trustee, but maybe the estate knows you're not the legal heir. I've been reading about estate law, and I was wondering if some sort of—" I stopped abruptly, because I thought he was having some kind of fit, and then realized he was laughing at me. "What?"

"You."

"I know I'm not magic. But I'm not completely useless."

"I know," he said, and his voice still held laughter, bright as sunshine. "You're always more than I expect, that's all.

Estate law. Christ."

We both fell quiet, and after several long minutes of nothing but the sounds of bees and cicadas, I turned my head to examine him. With all the tension gone from his face he looked—well, not quite healthy, but a fuller version of himself. Beads of sweat blossomed on his forehead and upper lip. I had a sudden vision of myself leaning over and kissing that lip, feeling his body rise under mine. Heat surged beneath my skin, unwelcome in the growing heat, and I threw it off like a heavy blanket.

"Preservation," he said suddenly.

"What?" I was still fighting off the firing of nerves in my limbs, and his voice made my insides quake.

His eyes were still closed, his face turned up to the sun. "I think that might be your magic. Keeping house, keeping growing things alive. It's subtle, but it's important." He turned his head to mine again. His eyes were clear blue. "Preservation. The keeping of good things."

WHEN I WENT to text my father that afternoon, I saw the girl again. Harmony, Suzy had said her name was.

I waved to her, and she waved back as she tread her way towards where I stood under the oak. I introduced myself, and she smiled at me.

"Suzy mentioned you," she said. Up close she looked even younger. Certainly not old enough to be a senior in high school, though of course Suzy had said she was. Perhaps I was just getting old. "You're the other hedge witch."

"Yes," I said. I didn't have the heart to explain. "But I'm new at it."

I put my hands against the fence that stood between us, and she mimicked me. She was barefoot again, and I wondered if that was somehow part of her technique.

"I was wondering," I said, "if you'd ever heard of a hedge witch breaking a curse."

She looked thoughtful. "Like a disease?"

"Maybe."

"I'm not sure. A hedge witch can only work with a natural process, not against it." She flexed her hands on the split rail fence. The tips of her fingers were stained green. "Corn is fully domesticated, but it's actually a grass. When I walk through the fields, I remind the corn what it's like to be a grass. It grows better that way. I'm not sure why." She winced, as though in apology. "What kind of disease?"

"The roses won't bloom."

"Do they have everything they need?"

It was the sort of question only an adolescent would ask—the innocence and presumption of a child, combined with the capabilities of an adult. Had I, an experienced gardener, thought of everything the roses needed to grow? Of course I had. And yet of course there was something I was missing. There had to be.

"I think so," I said. "It rains plenty, the soil is good. The house—" I paused, unsure of what I should or could share about the house. But Louis and Suzy had never forbidden *mention* of the place. "The house gives me wine, to spray the roses."

She frowned. "Is that a thing?"

I shrugged. "Not that I've heard of."

"But aren't you supposed to drink wine?"

"Yes, but—"

Wine for roses.

Of course. *Of course* the house had intended the wine to be drunk. And Louis had gone on and on about plants' ability to absorb—and I had been so stupid.

I thanked her and wandered away with a sense of strange, oncoming cheer. Ebullience, even. The roses would bloom. We could go home. Suzy could bring her students to the estate and show them the house. How pleased Colonel Mustard would be to have a rotating roster of guests to impress! The thought made me giddy.

Louis would be free. The roses would bloom, and he could leave the garden, leave the estate. He could leave the estate *with me*. I could take him home to my father's house—my house—and show him what a real rose garden could be like, covered in blooms and without a curse to weigh it down.

I ran back into the residence and down to the cellar. The light was on, as usual. I grabbed as many bottles as I could carry at once and hurried back up the cellar steps, wiping away the bottle dust on my jeans as I went. I grabbed a corkscrew from the butler's pantry.

Wine for roses.

In the garden, I poured a healthy shot for each plant, and when the bottle was empty, I opened another. While I worked, I sang the Spanish lullabies my mother used to sing to me. The ones I had sung to the roses as a child when I couldn't sleep. I breathed onto the leaves. I worked barehanded because I had to handle the bottles and corkscrew, and when the plants grabbed at the backs of my hands with their thorns, I let them have my blood too.

I gave the roses everything I could, until I couldn't think of anything else to give, and then I took the final half-empty bottle upstairs with me and drank directly from it on my balcony. When the wine had fizzed into my veins in a way that made me feel like pacing, like dancing, I jumped up and wound my way down the flagstone path to the man in the garden house below.

EIGHT

"ETHAN."

I had startled him. His eyes were wary as they scanned my face, searching for the emergency. In the daylight, as always, his face appeared wan and sickly.

I thought I had never seen a face I liked more.

He stepped aside to let me in. The hearth was empty, as it always was lately. Louis was no longer cold. He stood with his hands in his pockets, watching me like I was a wild animal, a predator in the rose garden whose patterns of behavior were unknown but likely to be erratic.

I grinned. "Do you feel a hundred years old?"

The strange expression cleared and he pursed his lips. "You smell like wine."

"Only a glass," I lied. "I brought more, though."

"Mm. I'll make us tea."

"We can open this." I held up the picnic basket that had

been waiting in the butler's pantry. The Colonel, as always, had anticipated my every need. "It feels like the Colonel packed us a bottle."

Louis blinked at me a moment as if judging my seriousness. "Tea," he said again and went off to futz with the kettle in the kitchen.

I perused the bookshelves that lined the walls. In fact, I'd had the equivalent of at least two glasses of wine on an empty stomach, and the effects were curious. I felt both unburdened of myself and as though I were hanging off the edge of a precipice with nothing but a fraying rope to hold on to. The temptation was to let go and see what happened.

I pulled a book down. The cover was dark blue and heavily battered. Stamped in gold letters were the words *Vegetable Gardening with an Affinity*. The copyright date on the title page was 1927.

Louis reappeared with a kettle in one hand and two mugs in the other. He settled himself on the sofa next to me. Our knees were a hand's breadth apart.

"One hundred years," I said again. "Do you feel like an old man?"

He sputtered as he handed me my cup, and his knee brushed mine. "I don't know. I don't change. The brain is only another organ, and my body's organs don't age. So I still feel like a young man." He took a sip of the tea. "I still make a young man's mistakes."

I drank deeply. The tea was a relief after the wine. I held up the vegetable gardening book and raised an eyebrow.

"I once hired a vegetable hedge witch," he said.

I laughed. "What for?"

He shrugged. "He was a hobo named Billy Chicago. At

least that's what he called himself. This was during the height of the Depression. All kinds of people were out of work, but most who passed through at that time were men like Billy, riding the rails and looking for work. I hired almost every hedge witch I encountered, whatever their affinity. And there were a lot of them, over the decades. I think that they were drawn here—*are* drawn here. The garden pulls what it needs towards itself."

"And the garden needed Billy."

"He taught me what he knew about gardening, the little he *knew* that he knew. He lost his factory job after the market crash. It was while he was on the move that he noticed he had uncanny foraging abilities. He could spot things others didn't, edible vegetation that grew wild. By the time I met him, he could charm a tomato plant into giving ripe fruit by early May."

"And you didn't fall in love with him?"

His head snapped up, incredulous. "He was sixty years old!" Then he saw that I was laughing at him. "Prick."

"Were none of them ever your lovers?"

He tilted his head. "Most of them were women, actually."

"You mentioned youthful mistakes."

He coughed, and his complexion mottled. "Ah. That was not the kind of mistake I was thinking of."

"I'm here," I said. "If you want to tell me anything."

He cleared his throat and turned toward me on the sofa, our hips farther apart, our knees pressed together. Angles in motion. "I've read—everything. It was how I survived for so long. And I loved it. I thought I was given a gift. Time enough to master absolutely any subject. The world didn't want men like me, but I could learn everything about the world in turn. I could conquer it. I hired hedge witches until I knew every type of hearth magic and garden magic. I read books on every subject, learned about atom bombs and shipping logistics and architecture. I became obsessed with the garden, with keeping it healthy, keeping it alive, because as long as it lived, so did I. But it grew wilder, and the blooms stopped coming. You know that part."

I did. I nodded. I did not interrupt.

"I became bitter without realizing it. I went on as before. I hired Suzy—that was ten years ago—but by then, I didn't care about anything she had to teach. I wasn't willing to face what was coming."

"Nothing is coming," I said. "I've had an idea. Actually, I was given an idea by multiple people, but I've finally learned to listen. I'm going to make the roses bloom."

He looked at me with his lips softly parted. Slowly, as if I were worth looking at. As if I were special. "You walked in one afternoon and it was like waking from a dream. I remembered that I wanted to live. That I was more than just a mind." His thin hand rested on his vibrating knee. I had only to reach out and take it. "That was my mistake," he said. "To have hope. It's why being near you makes me so afraid."

I put my hand on his, and his leg stilled. "Do you want me to leave?"

"No," he said. He looked down at our hands like they were a book he couldn't read. "But I'm so afraid."

It was funny, I thought, the way that fear didn't preclude any other emotion. Louis looked up from our hands to my face, and it was *him*. The man in the garden house who hated sweet wine and liked savory pies and lit fires in the middle of summer. The fear did not disappear. But something pulsed beneath it, some unanswered question to which I needed the answer. Oh, I craved it the way the roses craved sunlight.

"Well then," I said softly. "I could stay."

His lips parted again, but he said nothing. I reached for his mug, and he let me lift it from his hands. His empty fingers reached for me, clutching at my shirt. And when his body bent towards mine, I leaned in to meet it.

"Stay," he said against my lips.

I crushed back against him, like I could give myself to him, the way I had given myself to the roses. In the thin space between his chest and mine, there was no room for reality to intrude.

"I'll stay," I promised as I slid my hands round his waist and pulled him close. "I'll see the roses bloom."

I WOKE TO sunlight filtering in through the diamond panes of the dormer window. For a moment my mind floated untethered, blissfully blank. When I remembered that I was in the upper room of the garden house, I turned my face into the pillow. My heart raced, but my head felt clear, and a strange sensation burgeoned upwards, unfurling like a rose in the morning light.

Happy. I was happy. My lips curled into the pillow, and I rode the wave of feeling like a child rides an inner tube down a hill in winter, with gleeful terror, as though it were the very first time, already eager to drag the tube to the top of the hill and begin again.

When was the last time I was truly happy? If you had asked me before that summer, I would have said, before my diagnosis. Before my father's injury, before my mother's death. So many lines in the sand, each another mile marker between me and the happy childhood I had left behind. But that morning I thought—pruning the roses with my father in spring. Unloading groceries with Suzy in the kitchen. Louis lying in the grass, his face bright with the sun.

And Louis was the reason for my happiness that morning. It was the happiness of caring for another human being, and of being cared for. The fluttering excitement of new love. My heart pounded at the word. Was it love? Was it possible to love someone I'd known for only a few weeks, someone I was only just beginning to open myself up to?

The room was silent save the early morning bird chatter muted by the window. No sound came from my bedmate, and I rolled over to look for him. Bare to the waist, he lay on his side facing away from me. His ribs moved up and down steadily, sliding smoothly under the skin.

I hadn't realized Louis's breathing sounded so easy in sleep. He stirred, and I put a hand on his shoulder.

"Good morning," I said.

He rolled towards me, and my blood turned to ice.

He was—still him, still too thin, golden hair underwritten by implausibly milky-white skin. But he was beautiful. The sort of person I'd have been frightened to even talk to at school. An Adonis who had whatever number and gender of admirers he preferred trailing after him at all times through the quad, a god in whose temple I could never hope to worship.

He sat up, and I saw that his chest was broader, his shoulders straighter. His golden hair was full and healthy, his complexion luminous. A rose in full bloom.

"Ethan? What's wrong?"

His voice was both his and not. His chest was no longer concave, his lungs no doubt healthier. My Louis had been such a sickly thing. This Louis looked like the young man in the portrait, the one in the greenhouse I had covered up in disgust. Of course he did. Because Louis was Aloysius Kilbride, the heir to the estate. God, I was so stupid. The heir had been in the garden house all along.

"Ah," I said, unintelligently. I scrubbed my hands over my face, but when I looked up, the handsome stranger was still there, a look of concern furrowing his beautiful brow. On a lesser man it would have marred his features. On him I wanted to memorize it, to touch my fingers to the creased muscle like precious marble.

"I feel," he said slowly, as though testing the taste of the new voice in his mouth, "strange." He looked down at his hands and turned them over back to front. The lines of his veins were no longer quite so visible, his flesh no longer quite so thin. Highlights of gold shone where the morning sun hit his hair. "I feel good."

I curled my fingers into my palms and squeezed until my fingernails bit into the skin like thorns. He had lied to me. "That's—good. That's good."

He looked up at me again with understanding on his face. If I thought confusion had looked handsome on him then sympathy was like being gazed upon by angels. "Ethan," he said again in that wonderful, adorable voice.

I threw back the covers. "I have to spray the roses. It's

late, I didn't mean to sleep so long."

"It's only seven. Stay." He reached for me, but I shrank back, and his hand fell to the bed.

"I can't. I need to—I also need to call my dad, and of course Suzy will be here today, so I need to get everything done early." I grabbed my shirt. My fingers stumbled on the buttons a few times. It was the same shirt, I realized, the same blood-red Rob Roy I had been wearing the night he pulled me out of the rain. Back when he had been himself and not the stranger beside me.

Before I slipped out of the room, I chanced a backwards glance. His eyes were still focused on his hands, watching them in fascination.

He had lied to me. I kicked at the gravel on the path back to the main house.

I decided to check on my baby roses again before starting my other chores, and I was glad I did. The new roots had finally stabilized the plants, and they stood taller, plump-stemmed and bushy-leafed. I busied myself watering them and debated getting them more wine. I didn't want to overdo it. They were, after all, just babies.

Every time Louis' new face intruded in my thoughts, I pushed it away. But it returned, again and again, relentless. I was so preoccupied, I didn't notice the difference at the end of the stems right away. And then I thought I was imagining it.

I touched a plant with trembling fingers.

My baby rose had—buds. The bud fell from my fingertips as I reached for the next plant, which like its sister boasted a single bud at the end of what had been—what I had thought was—a blind shoot.

I raced through the greenhouse door, back through the house and into the garden. The first plants I came upon were a row of mosses, their fuzzy greenery ruddy in the sunlight. They were short, almost a ground cover, lining the front of the bed. I fell to my knees in the dirt—and found buds. And not immature buds either, but buds already tinged with color at the tips. A shocking suggestion of pink amidst all the endless greens and browns and rusts of the garden.

Buds, everywhere I walked.

Each and every plant was laden with buds. Some small and just beginning, others just barely visible, emerging from the new growth at the end of stems. Still others with sepals already pulled away and heady with a tinge of color, ready to burst. I had missed them—or not noticed—or they had come up overnight. Some of the varietals I was able to identify by the color, while in other cases I realized I must have been mistaken and was forced to reassess.

I sat down in the Temple of Aphrodite and watched as the Madame waved tiny bud-lets in the breeze. My heart rate slowly stabilized, leaving me alone with my thoughts. The roses had buds. They would bloom any day, and the garden would be magnificent again. Just as Louis was magnificent. Again his face flooded my mind, and I felt almost ashamed at how much I wanted him. It felt like reaching for something I had not earned.

The roses would bloom, and Louis would be free.

And I would go home.

I AVOIDED THE garden house the rest of the morning. Suzy was late and I missed lunch, but when the light slanted towards late afternoon I could no longer ignore my stomach. I made my way to the butler's pantry where a picnic basket waited expectantly in the dumbwaiter.

"Yes, alright," I said irritably and set off for the garden house. In a few days—a week perhaps—a walk in the garden in the late afternoon would be nothing short of heavenly. Along the way, I cut a dozen of the most promising stems I could find, their sepals already peeling away and tips tinged with promised color. Proof of my double fee. My ticket home.

Louis answered the door with a smile that wilted as he took in my face. I found a pitcher in the kitchen for the roses and arranged them haphazardly, a medley of sizes and colors and shapes. It wouldn't be beautiful. It would be wild, like an English rose garden should be.

In the sitting room, Louis laid out the picnic spread, which that afternoon prominently featured corn. Corn butter rice, cold corn chowder, and a golden curry loaded with corn and tofu and summer squash. And of course, wine. A white to complement the vegetables. Louis watched me out of the corner of his eye as he poured the wine, which made me feel like a rabid dog, untrustworthy and unpredictable.

I set my makeshift vase on the cold hearth. "Nearly everything is in bloom. I cut a few varieties, so you can get a sense of what's out there."

He glanced down at the bowl. "They'll die in here."

"Yes," I said. "But they'll bloom slowly first, and you'll be able to enjoy them."

He nodded solemnly. He had combed his hair so that it swept back from his forehead, very unlike how I had left him, with his hair tumbled from sleep. It was still long, but it was thick and full, and he looked like the jazz-age movie star he ought to have been.

I cleared my throat. "I expect the best of the flush will be in about a week or two, if the weather holds. The garden—"

"Damn the garden. Ethan. Talk to me. Tell me what I did wrong."

My throat felt as though the muscles were stuck together, and I had to cough again before I could speak. "Why didn't you tell me your real name?"

Whatever he had been expecting, it wasn't that. His mouth fell open for a beat before he answered. "Louis is my name. My parents named me Aloysius, as in St. Aloysius Gonzaga—Luigi Gonzaga. They were Catholic, and rather pretentious about using it to connect with the common voter."

"I'd've liked to have known I was working for you."

"You don't. You work for the estate, and I don't own it," he said shortly. "I was disinherited."

"I saw the portrait."

He paled, but his jaw was set. "I never meant to lie to you, Ethan. I just... I met you, and there was no reason to tell you. Then we were—" He stopped. "I convinced myself it didn't matter."

"Of course it matters," I said. "I've been trying to break the curse, and you haven't even told me who you really are."

His mouth fell open. He looked like I'd hit him. "You what?"

"The curse," I said angrily. The tension was still rattling around in my body, looking for an escape hatch. "Isn't that what you hired me to do? Make the roses bloom? Jesus, you must have thought I was an idiot."

"Of course not. Ethan, I never expected you to—"

"So I'm what? Not one of your hedge witches, a second-rate gardener at best. A toy, something to assuage your loneliness—"

"Yes," he said sharply, with a flash of anger. His handsome face flushed. "I was lonely. I was sick and tired of being alone, with no one but a cat and whomever I could pay to keep company. Then you came along, someone I hadn't even meant to hire, someone I hadn't been looking for, like a goddamn miracle, and suddenly I wasn't lonely anymore. I saw no reason to scare you off."

The air between us heaved and rolled. But his anger had deflated mine and left me cold. "If I were going to be scared off," I said calmly, "it would have been the night I witnessed you torture yourself on a thorn bush."

He exhaled through his nose. "I asked you to help the roses bloom. I never asked you to break the curse."

I stared at him, agape. "But that's what the bloom will do, won't it? Won't the bloom break the curse?"

He looked at me helplessly.

"What happens when I leave?" I said.

"The roses will bloom. And then they will die."

Of course. They would bloom like the once-a-summer plants they were, and then the blooms would wilt and shatter, leaving behind nothing but discarded petals and burgeoning rose hips. "And after that?"

He shook his head, slowly. "I don't know."

"Right."

"Ethan—"

But whatever he would have said was cut off by the alien sound of a ringtone. And it was coming from my pocket. "But... there's no service." I pulled out the phone, which despite my declaration displayed two small bars and a green incoming call. Kay.

I lifted the phone to my ear. "Aunt Kay? What's wrong, is Dad okay?"

"I'm fine, thank you." Her testy voice came through clear. "And it's not an emergency, no one's in the hospital. But I'm at your father's house. I tried you an hour ago, but it went to voicemail."

"What happened?"

"Relapse. Started about a week ago, and it's gotten worse. Doc gave him some meds but otherwise didn't seem too concerned."

I exhaled slowly. If the doctor wasn't concerned—and if Kay's interpretation of *concerned* could be relied upon— then it couldn't be too bad yet.

"Then he fell yesterday," Kay continued.

"What—Jesus, Kay, why didn't you open with that?"

Across the room, Louis's head flicked up.

"Don't you swear at me, young man. He broke his collar-bone. It'll heal just fine, but he needs to keep his right arm immobilized for a little while, which is hard enough in his position. He tried to call you too."

I closed my eyes as though I could block out her words and the look of concern on Louis' face.

"Look, Ethan. My stubborn ass of a brother wouldn't want me to say this to you, but I think you should come home."

"I—yes, of course. I can be there tonight. Where is he right now?"

"Sleeping. I'll let him know you're on your way if he wakes up."

I thanked her and ended the call. My call history showed that I had indeed missed her about an hour ago. And several hours before that, I had missed a call from my father.

I looked up to see Louis watching me, ashen faced.

"My father," I said unnecessarily. "He's hurt. I have to go."

He nodded and glanced toward the front window, through which the long afternoon daylight still shone. "Go quickly. I'll have Suzy send along anything you've forgotten, and your payment."

My hands were shaking. I clenched them into fists, feeling the fingernails pierce my skin. "Louis—I'll come back."

"You've done everything expected of you."

"I said I'd stay to see the roses bloom," I said, but he had already turned away, looking at the pitcher of buds. "I promised."

A truck horn barked, startling both of us. "There's Suzy," he said. "If you get her to jump your truck, you can be home before dark."

He hesitated, looking as though he were on the verge of saying something else. Then he swallowed and said, "Thank you. For my mother's garden."

NINE

I THREW MY potted baby roses and duffel into the bed of the truck, then flung myself into the driver's seat. The engine sputtered just long enough to stop my heart, but finally the ancient cylinders roared to life.

"That's right, beautiful." I stroked a hand down the cracked leather of the steering wheel.

Suzy climbed out of her truck and disconnected the jumper cables. "Might as well head out directly. It'll be good for the battery to drive it. Text me when you're at your dad's."

"I will. Thanks, Suzy."

She paused for a moment, her hand resting on the open window of my cab. Then she said, "Be good."

I left the Kilbride Estate behind with a spit of gravel.

Kay's white sedan was parked in our driveway when I got home, so I parked the truck on the street and walked up to the side door. It was locked. I huffed in frustration and started to dig for my keys, but the door swung open. Kay stood on the threshold, her thick gray hair shining like a halo in the light from the kitchen. I blinked.

She frowned as only she could, with her whole face, lips and brow and eyes turned down. "Did they not let you shower at this fancy place?"

"Hi, Aunt Kay." I shoved past her with my duffel. I'd left the roses in the truck bed for the time being. "Where's Dad?"

She closed the door behind me and locked it, something my father and I never bothered with if one of us was home. "Asleep, probably for the night. The doctor gave him some painkillers."

I nodded, not bothering to hide my disappointment. I felt like a sullen teenager again. "I'll just head up and shower, then."

Kay looked at me sharply. "You eaten?"

"I—" I was about to say yes when I remembered that I hadn't actually eaten anything in the dinner basket the Colonel prepared. I had a brief vision of Louis standing over the spread and contemplating the corn cakes alone. "No."

"There's a casserole in the fridge, grab yourself a plate and nuke it."

While I dished out a serving of tan-colored mush and microwaved it, Kay filled me in on the details. My father had been experiencing a flare up for a few days, and his problems walking had worsened. Yesterday he tripped on the wooden steps that led up to our side door. Such a small thing, and yet. He was able to get himself up but had to call an ambulance when he realized he couldn't lift his right arm.

"He was lucky, you know," Kay said. She sat at the table while I ate and watched every bite I took as if taking inventory. I wondered if she planned to record it in her strange tally of who-owes-what in the family accounting book. "The doctor said as much. The sclerosis has been fairly mild."

"Lucky," I said. "Broken bones don't seem very lucky."

Kay's eyes narrowed. She was a few years younger than my father, and I was surprised at how obvious the difference was. I hadn't seen her in a few years, though she invited us up to South Bend every year for Thanksgiving. Too busy, my father always said.

"None of us get out alive, you know. Think you'd be more grateful that God and family are looking out for your father. Not everyone is so fortunate."

I returned silently to my casserole, which turned out to be a soggy tuna-melt Kay must have made. Lucky, fortunate. It was hard to pretend to be a good and grateful Christian when the Christian across the table was berating you. I had a vague idea that Kay had left the Catholic Church for some big-box born-again affair, but that didn't mean she didn't still layer everything with a healthy dose of Catholic guilt.

"Your father said you got a job on a fancy estate for the summer."

"Gardener," I said, thinking that if I kept my answers to as few syllables as possible she would pick up on the fact that I didn't want to talk.

She didn't. "Good. I've always said that you needed a real

job. If the business goes under then you'll need another source of income. I'm guessing this will help with the debt?"

I looked at her, a bite of cheesy fish still halfway to my mouth.

Kay raised her eyebrows. "Your father told me about the hospital payment plan."

I hadn't realized that my father presented his request for a loan as anything other than business. But he would have had to explain why his insurance was so terrible, the deductible so high, why he was so reluctant to go to a doctor before things got worse.

"I've always said something like this could happen, that he should give up the stupid rose-hunting business or whatever it is. Real jobs have health insurance, a steady paycheck, security." She shook her head. "You and your father should be grateful that you have me available at a moment's notice."

Grateful. Yes, I ought to be grateful to Kay. I was so grateful my father was sick, that he was hurt. That I had to leave a job I loved, a man I cared for—a man I maybe even loved—so that I could go home and take care of my father the way I would for the rest of his life.

My stomach twisted. Was I—had I been—bitter?

I loved my father. I wanted to take care of him. But in choosing to come home, I had left something else behind.

I put more tuna in my mouth, one dutiful forkful after another. When my plate was empty, I put down my fork and stood up. "I'm going to go shower."

"You don't want more?"

"No, thanks."

"Take that dish to the sink. And go softly on the stairs, not your usual lumbering, you don't want to wake your dad. Leave your duffel here, I'll wash your things."

Her loud voice was more likely to wake my father than I was, but I obediently took my plate to the sink and scraped off the cheese under the running water.

Behind me Kay was unzipping my duffel, throwing my dirty things down the laundry chute. I cringed, thinking of her touching my clothes, feeling a degree of exposure that seemed out of step with the situation. And then I remembered the last time I had seen Kay. My grandmother's funeral. I was sixteen, and we went up to South Bend for the funeral mass. Afterwards, at the burial, I let a few tears slip down my face, and Kay told me to stop crying and man up. My father had overheard and told her to jump in St. Joseph's river. We hadn't seen her much after that. Because my father hadn't tolerated anyone mistreating me.

The plate slipped from my hands and landed in the sink with a clatter. I gripped the edge of the counter, blinking back hot tears.

"Ethan? Are you alright?"

I looked over my shoulder. Kay stood at the opposite side of the kitchen, my empty duffel in her hands and what may have been genuine concern on her face. I stared at her a beat too long, and her expression turned from concern to something like fear.

"Just tired," I said. The tap was still running. I shut it off and left the plate where it had fallen, then dried my hands on the dish towel. "I'm going to bed."

WHEN I CAME downstairs the next morning it was already full daylight. My father was sitting at the kitchen table, a smile on his face and a steaming cup of coffee next to the hand that wasn't caught up in a sling. His cane hung off the edge of the table.

"Morning, lazybones." He nodded at the coffee pot, which held more than enough for three caffeine-addicted people. So Kay had told him I was coming. I poured myself a cup from the ancient carafe and slid onto the bench opposite him. He was still wearing his pajamas, but he had an open fleece zip-up slung loosely over his shoulders.

"Aunt Kay awake?" I asked.

He shook his head. "Up at the crack of dawn myself."

"Well, you did sleep for twelve hours."

He gave me a look that meant I was a little shit. I grinned into my coffee.

There was no Kay, no roses, no diseases or broken bones—only me, my father, and the coffee. I closed my eyes and let the steam from my cup slowly melt the ice in my chest. It felt like dawn. I had been deprived of the sun too long and it felt good, so good, to be back where I belonged.

It was almost perfect. But.

Where my father's house would have once welcomed me home, just as Colonel Mustard made sure I felt at home at the Kilbride Estate, an emptiness reverberated. A ghost of sensation, manifest only in its absence.

"You okay?"

My father was watching me with a curious expression on his face.

"Of course," I said. "How are you? How's the—" I gestured towards my collarbone.

He inclined his head towards his good shoulder, a subtle motion that avoided moving his upper chest. "Throbs a bit," he said in an understated tone. He wasn't being brave. He would have said if it hurt. But he was also far too used to pain. He pointed with his chin out the window. "Found those in the truck."

Sitting outside on the back porch were the three baby roses in their pots. They looked healthy. Ready for transfer.

"Where'd they come from?" My father asked.

And I remembered, suddenly, that I had never asked for permission to take them home. "I think I stole them," I said.

My father grunted into his coffee. "Ah, well."

"I'll plant them tomorrow. I thought one or two would look good climbing the back door."

"Hmm." He squinted out the window. "What are they?"

"The Madame," I said quietly. "They have buds."

"No shit," he said. He looked impressed. He rustled carefully in his jacket pocket with his good arm and withdrew an envelope. "I also found this in the mailbox." He tossed the envelope across the table and it landed in front of me with a thwack.

It had no postage stamp or address, just my name written across the front. Inside was a stack of bills half an inch thick. I slid it out and fanned them open. Hundreds, all of them.

I looked up. "There are thousands of dollars here."

"Ten grand," my father confirmed.

"Ten gr—"

"Five more envelopes just like it. This was with them." He slid a flat, square envelope across the table. Inside was another flat card with words written in the same elegant script as my name:

For the roses — L

"Is it from him?" My father asked.

I nodded, numb. Suzy must have dropped them off. I wondered if she even knew what was inside. Sixty grand. More than enough to pay down our bills.

My father sat back and blew the air out of his lungs, then winced. "It's a hell of a salary for two months' labor."

"They bloomed," I said. "Or were just about to. Yesterday, they had buds. Every single plant." I swallowed. "That's why it's so much money. A double fee if the roses bloomed. That's what he promised."

"Well, we'll have to talk to the bank. There's paperwork involved for this much cash."

I laughed, a nervous, bubbly reaction. Of course there was paperwork. There would always be paperwork and taxes. The hallmarks of the normalcy I had been thrust back into.

Because I wouldn't be going back to the Kilbride Estate. I might never see Louis again.

The feeling of lightness solidified and became a mass somewhere in the vicinity of my larynx.

"That's good," my father said slowly. "It is good, right?"

"Of course it's good, it's—it's sixty fucking grand."

Footsteps creaked from upstairs, and soon came the sound of running water.

"I'm so sorry, Dad," I said.

"Sorry? What the hell for? Bringing home sixty grand?"

I shook my head. My throat was thick. "For not being here. If I had gotten your call—"

"I would've told you not to worry," he said firmly. "I had

already called Kay, she was on her way down when I called you to let you know what was going on." He scowled. "It was my own damn fault. I knew I didn't have the balance, but I didn't want to break out the cane." He rapped the head of the cane with a knuckle, and it swung in response. "Wasn't ready."

I bit my lip hard and nodded. I couldn't cry. Not when Kay would be down any minute.

My father was still watching me closely. "How are you feeling? Have you had any—"

"No," I said quickly. "No, I've been fine."

"If you're sure," he said unhappily.

"Honest, I've been fine, I just..." I lost my voice and stared down into my coffee. I had come home after extended periods away only twice in my life, and each time it was because my father had been hurt.

I hadn't even realized I was crying until I felt tear drops on my hands.

"It's alright," my father said roughly. "It's a lot, I get it. Don't worry about Kay, she can go to hell."

I laughed. The sound was watery. "She did come help you."

"Yeah, so she could lord it over me for the next ten years." He picked up the cane and tapped it on the floor. "Ain't exactly altruism."

"You know perfectly well I can hear you, Arthur," said Kay. She strode into the kitchen and over to where we sat. My father grimaced but lifted his face, and Kay kissed him on the cheek.

I swiped at my cheeks with my sleeves.

"Good morning, Ethan," she said as she straightened.

"Thank you for defending me to this stubborn ass here."

"Morning, Aunt Kay."

My father rolled his eyes when Kay turned her back to reach for the coffee. She poured herself a generous cup. Egregious amounts of coffee was the one vice all my family members shared. I thought of Louis drinking tea alone in the garden house. I pushed the thought away.

Kay stirred a heaping spoonful of sugar into her coffee and began putting away dishes like she had lived in our house for years. "Arthur, you have an appointment at ten today."

My father frowned. "I thought the doctor said next week."

"Not with the doctor, the physical therapist. We're going out to Fort Wayne, to the specialist she recommended."

"I'll take you, Dad," I said, but he shook his head.

"There's actually a few things I'd like you to take care of around the house, if you don't mind. Kay'll take me."

"That's right, she will," Kay said. "Even if you are an ingrate. Finish your coffee and come up and get real clothes on, Arthur. Don't forget your cane."

She banged the silverware drawer closed and bustled out of the room.

My father grimaced again and looked down at his coffee. "She's not so bad, really."

I shot him a look that meant, *I don't believe you.*

"She's been helpful. But there are a few things I can only ask you to do. Deadheading and the like. The garden is way overdue."

"Of course, Dad."

"And in the meantime, if you wouldn't mind throwing a

load of laundry in. I'd ask Kay, but..."

I knew what he meant. I'd already had the humiliation of Kay going through my dirty things.

"No reason to rush." He leaned on his cane and used it to push himself up out of the booth. "We've got all day."

"Aunt Kay said your appointment is at ten."

He frowned at the clock on the microwave, which said eight twenty. "Is that right, or did we never change it for daylight time?"

I laughed. "It's right. But you should get going anyway."

"Hope springs eternal." He left, his cane thunking softly along the linoleum.

I PLANTED MY baby Madames first. I figured two would do for over the door. The other I would train up and over the window by the breakfast nook. We had never planted anything there before, and to turn over the soil I first had to remove an odd assortment of old pavers and stones. Then I used a spade to soften the dirt and stir in a heap of compost, and I tucked my baby roses into the earth.

The color that peaked through the bud tips was odd—darker than I would have expected. Madame Alfred Carrière was a pale pink rose, nearly white, but the buds were almost crimson. But then, buds were typically darker than the eventual flower, and I wasn't very familiar with the Madame. Not a blooming one, anyway.

My father's rose farm felt strange after my time at the Kilbride Estate. Not quite an acre, his land was planted with several dozen varieties of reliably blooming roses, most of them the hybrid teas that sold well in grocery stores. Plus a few of the fluffier Austins popular with our florist clients who used them in wedding bouquets. Our farm was far more orderly than the romantic Victorian garden at the manor, laid out in neat rows designed for ease of access rather than aesthetics. But even so, I loved it. I had missed it. Bees and butterflies danced from blossom to blossom, lingering over the open blooms, the garden roses open like cups of nectar, revealing golden stamens.

The pollinators scattered lazily ahead of me, floating away and back again like bubbles on a breeze. Deadheading was especially important for roses that bloom continuously, since cutting off the wilting flowers told the plants to keep the new blooms coming. And that was essential, because new flowers were our primary source of income. It was not a good sign my father had let the deadheading get so far behind. Without the steady grocery store income, we'd get behind on our strict debt payment plan.

I shook my head as I stretched gloved hands into the plant in front of me. We had no more debt, or would have no more once my father dealt with the bank and the hospital. The business would survive. My father could grow his non-grocery store client list, and he would hunt down beautiful forgotten roses to cultivate, and I would give his roses wine.

We would move on.

I sat down between the rows just as I had as a boy, pretending I was invisible amongst the flowers. I used to imagine they could talk, like in *Alice in Wonderland*, and they would protect me like one of their own. In middle school when I was bullied for being gay, before I even really knew what that meant, the rows had been my hiding spot. Inside my family's house and my father's garden I built myself a castle, and it had protected me.

I wrapped my arms around my legs and let the August sun beat down on my head. It was nearing noon, the sun directly overhead, showering me in light and heat the same as any flower. When I lifted my arm to wipe the sweat from my forehead, the scent of roses clung to my shirt like a woman's perfume. I wondered if the stems I left in the garden house had started to open. I wondered if Louis had touched them, if he would go out to the garden and see the rest of the blooms. He could collect enough healthy buds to keep himself alive and well for another year, another season. Suzy would bring him groceries next year, and the years and decades after that, until the symbiosis between garden and man stretched to its breaking point and finally fell apart.

I dropped my head into my hands and let my father's house reach for me, pull me in, and hold me close.

MY FATHER GRAZED the crimson-tinged buds with his fingertips. "Odd," he said. "Are you sure this is a Madame Alfred Carrière?"

"I cut them from the same plant you brought home," I said uncertainly.

"Huh." He stood up slowly, one foot and then the other. "Well, I've never owned one." He winced as he reached for his cane. In the end, he needed the prescription painkillers. The physical therapy had been harder than he expected—especially the second session, which landed him in the BarcaLounger for the rest of the day—and he had spent the next several days working on pain management. But the third session went better, and by Friday he felt well enough that he asked me to take him out into the garden. I had been home for a week.

He gave the new plants a last curious look, and then we walked the rows, snipping off wilting blossoms as we went. He had to stop and rest the cane against his leg in order to pluck off the heads, so it was slow going.

It was the first time we had been together without Kay for a long stretch, and I told him everything. About the gardens and Louis, about the way the house brought me breakfast and tools and books, about Suzy and her hedge witch honey. About wine for roses. My father grunted occasionally but otherwise didn't say much. He even accepted the idea that a man had lived in a garden house for a hundred years with remarkably little surprise. But he frowned when I mentioned the wine.

"Wine for roses," he said. "I wouldn't have thought of that."

It was the same thing Louis had said months ago. "You've never heard of anyone doing that?"

He shrugged. "No, but that doesn't mean it's not a thing. Besides," he stopped to lean the cane against his thigh, "what kind of a hedge witch would I be if I couldn't learn from the one I trained?" He leaned over and twisted off a wilted flower with his ungloved fingers.

"I'm not a witch," I said.

My father stopped and turned around so quickly he

winced. "Not a witch? Where'd you get an idea like that?"

"I—I don't know. I've always known."

"Hmm." He twisted off another flower then grabbed his cane again. "Well, you would know better than me, I guess. But everything you told me—the house, the garden—sure sounds like magic to me. Didn't the roses bloom?"

"Yes, but that wasn't…"

"Wasn't what? You? Magic?"

Preservation, Louis had said. The keeping of good things. Just like a house, warm and welcoming.

"It was a curse," I said, a little desperately. "I was just—trying to break the curse."

"S'ok," my father said gruffly. "You have years to figure this stuff out. It's not like a job, or—or a marriage. Being a hedge witch, I mean. It's not even really a decision you have to make."

"I failed, in any case. I was trying to make the roses bloom because I thought that would break the curse. But it didn't. Louis lied to me about who he is. It was his parents' estate. That's how he became the trustee. He never told me."

"Bastard," my father said loyally.

"He's not—" I faltered. My father had met a petulant, sickly sort of man in a garden house, but that was not the man I had left. "He's not."

"Okay."

"He took my word for things. He let me do what I thought was best." Except, of course, for the diseased plant in the walled garden. But even so. "I loved it. The job, I mean. Even if—well. I didn't end things well, with Louis."

He stopped and looked at me. "Did he hurt you?"

"No!" I nearly barreled into him and stopped myself just

in time. "No, he would never hurt me."

My father scanned my face. "What happened?"

I brought my hand up to my hair before I remembered I was wearing gloves. I let the hand fall back to my side. "I don't know."

He was the most beautiful man I had ever seen and I couldn't bear to look at him. How did you explain something like that, much less to your own father? I couldn't explain how I was both attracted and repulsed. The way I wanted him, but the way I'd wanted the skinny man in the garden house too. The way the wanting had nothing to do with what he looked like and everything to do with who he was.

The way that I loved him and would never know if he felt the same way.

"Were you two..." My father waved a hand.

"No. Yes." I reconsidered. "We might have been. But there wasn't enough trust there, I think. There wasn't enough time."

"Ah." My father nodded. "Trust is important."

"I broke my promise." Hot shame coursed up my jaw, into my cheeks. "I promised I would stay to see the roses bloom. And I didn't, and I know I'm supposed to be here—I know that, Dad—and I don't know what to do."

My father sighed and turned back to his roses. He snapped a blown flower, then another.

"You know, there was a young priest in the parish where I grew up. Well, I guess he's an old fucker now, if he's still alive. He used to go on and on about vocation. Discernment. Figuring out what God wanted you to do. I think he actually meant the priesthood, but I took him at his word. I always figured I'd work in steel, like your grandfather. But I hated the thought of it, being stuck inside a factory all day. I liked the feel of dirt between my fingers, liked the way green things grew and bloomed. But I thought God wanted me in that factory. I felt messed up, so I did what we were supposed to do when we felt messed up: I went to confession. But the priest in the confessional that day was Father Merton, the monsignor. He's for sure dead by now. When I gave my confession, he just laughed at me. And he said, Art, what do *you* want to do? God can figure out the rest."

"I don't—what are you saying?"

"Ethan." My father stopped again to look at me. "What do you want?"

I thought of the man in the garden house. Louis in the garden. Louis by the fire with his fingers in my hair. Louis with his face turned up towards the sun.

"Do you love him?"

I clipped another flower from its stalk. It shattered in my hand, sending faded pink petals everywhere. I looked up at my father, who watched me with kind eyes.

He just smiled. "I booked another trip," he said.

"What?" The man had just suffered a broken collarbone, and he was already talking about traveling? I immediately began imagining everything that could go wrong if my father decided to start traveling alone again. "When? Should I come?"

He waved a hand. "Late next spring. June. I want to go out west, take a look at a few more of those estates. All with permission, of course. No more trespassing."

"Oh," I said. "And do you want me to go?"

He shrugged with his good shoulder. "Maybe. We'll see. In the meantime, I'll make sure that I spend this winter getting healthy. Doing my therapy, that sort of thing. And—Kay said she wanted to go. To take a look at the roses. If you're busy, or you don't want to."

"Dad, I don't mind. You know I don't."

His mouth tightened at the corners.

"Dad, I love roses. I do. I always have. I spent all summer with roses. It was—" Wonderful, impossible, terrifying, warm. Louis lying in the sun. Louis lying in bed.

"Alright," he said gently. "I believe you. E, look, you deserve your own life. That's my only point. I don't say that to kick you out. You're not my employee, you're my partner. Hell, you don't have to decide anything now. But if this is what you want, there will always be a place here for you. You do your thing. It'll keep."

THAT AFTERNOON I fixed the wobbly kitchen table leg and set out the old Clue board, which I had found crammed into the upstairs closet. Astonishingly, it appeared to have most of the pieces. My father laughed when he saw the board set up on the kitchen table, and I made popcorn and popped open three beers. Kay joined us for one game, which she won, then announced she was tired and went to bed.

As she rinsed her beer bottle and put it by the sink, I felt it again. My family's house, come back to life. It shimmered at me, just a gentle *hello*. The familiarity rushed through me like the first cool breeze of autumn. A nostalgia made of family and board games and comfort.

My father and I played three more games. Clue isn't

really made for two players, but over the years we had worked out house rules that made it possible for the two of us when my mother had gotten so sick of the game, and then eventually so sick, that she couldn't play. It had the effect of making the game longer, and after three rounds it was nearly midnight.

"I should go to bed." I rubbed my hand over my face and blinked out at the shadows of the Madames I had planted. They were doing well, and I had already set the first peg into the doorframe to encourage them to climb.

My father swept up the Clue cards with one hand. "What time you heading out?"

"Early. I expect I'll be back by dinner, but I'll text you either way. There's plenty of leftovers in the fridge, so you should be able to manage, and—"

"E," my father said sternly. "I'm a goddamn adult, and I've got Kay. Go for as long as you need."

I hesitated. "I'm just going to see what I can work out. Clean up and—well, there won't be much to do. I just want to keep my promise."

Because I loved Louis. I was sure of it. I still didn't know what I wanted out of life. Not really. I only knew that I wanted to build something together like my parents had done. I wanted to build a home.

We put away the game. I showered so I wouldn't have to in the morning and then lay awake in bed. The mattress was old and lumpy. It sank too much beneath my weight and put my spine at a weird angle. I shifted uncomfortably for a while, listening to my father's shuffling noises, which eventually turned to soft snores. I shifted and flipped my pillow, trying to ignore the growing ache in my back. After twenty more minutes, I gave up.

It was late, but it was a full moon, and the backyard was bright. The palest roses looked nearly phosphorescent in the moonlight, and I caressed their velvet petals as I passed. By early morning they would be covered with dew.

I made a lap around the commercial rows to burn off some energy then headed back towards the house where the garden roses grew. I sat on the step next to the Madames. At the top of the plant, one of the buds had finally burst open. I grinned and reached out to gently touch it. In the darkness, I didn't notice at first what I surely would have seen immediately in the daylight. My father's other pale roses glowed beneath the moon. This bloom did not glow. It didn't look pale at all.

I dug my phone out of my pocket and used the screen as a light.

The rose was a deep, passionate pink. The color the sky took on the morning of a rainstorm. The faded color of my red pickup. A color that was no longer quite so fashionable in the rose world. Too flamboyant for a wedding, too gaudy for a truly tranquil garden.

I began to laugh. It wasn't a Madame at all. I had no idea what it was. The excitement rose in me, slowly at first, and then bubbling so fast that I had to quell the urge to go and wake my father immediately.

He needed sleep.

And the roses would still be blooming in the morning.

TEN

"WHAT IS IT?"

The next morning, my father stood on the steps of the back porch and frowned down at the not-Madames planted around the door. Each sported a few blossoms fully open in the morning sun, their deep crustacean-pink as startling as it had been last night.

"I have no idea," I said honestly. "Any guesses?"

My father knelt carefully, one hand on the stair railing for balance. He reached out a few shaking fingers and grazed the nearest flower. The cutting he brought home, the same plant from which I propagated these, had been nearly white. A lot of flowers changed color with the weather or other conditions. But looking down at the Madame, I wondered if the plant had been in disguise. As if it weren't yet sure we could be trusted.

But maybe, I thought, my father had known all along.

Even if he had called it a Madame. Perhaps it had bloomed pink for him and the memory had faded with the rose as he got farther from the estate. Maybe my father's magic, his rose rustler's blood, had called him to this plant, to this rose.

He looked up at me, blinking, as if into the sun. His mouth hung open a little. As though I were the witch.

My father laughed.

THE SUN WAS halfway up the sky by the time I turned off the 31 and bumbled down the road along the edge of the windmill forest. When I found the service path that led to the Kilbride Estate, I began to speed, my heart pounding, until my tires hit the familiar gravel crunch of the drive.

It was quiet—a familiar quiet, the peace of the estate at midday, when it was too hot for most wildlife and the atmosphere seemed to shimmer with the promise of more heat to come. But the drive looked funny. Weeds grew thick and threatening out of the gravel, nettles up past my ankles, dandelions blown. These were not plants that had come up in a week. Had whatever magic that sped up the roses affected these too?

I pulled my father's shovel from the truck bed and threw it over my shoulder like a knight storming into battle. The front door of the house came slowly, stickily. As though it had not been opened in a long time. The foyer was dark, and no lights came on in the house as I entered. The upper story gaped, a dark maw above the grand staircase. I opened my mouth to call for the Colonel, and my lungs filled with dust.

I flew to the back of the house. The kitchen stood dark and still, the chef's table covered in a quarter inch of dust. I was afraid I had somehow dreamed the whole thing. That the garden had convinced me I had lived in luxury for nine weeks and met a man named Louis in the garden house.

Most of all, I was afraid to go into the gardens.

I pushed open the door in the butler's pantry and walked beneath the shadowed trellis. The vines that climbed over the latticework were brown and dead. At the far end, the sunlight dazzled the garden from view. I held my heart in my throat and took one step, then another, blinded by sunlight, until at last I found myself in my rose garden.

Most of the roses were already blown, rose hips burgeoning on the branch. The leaves had begun to yellow and drop, revealing bare canes full of teeth. The gravel paths were overrun with weeds and suckers. At least a full season's worth of unchecked growth and decay.

The wildest briars grew right up to the garden house like a demonic ground cover. They seemed to swallow it, converging on a central point on the second story as the thorns climbed the walls, completely blocking out the windows. I couldn't see the front door. It looked like Sleeping Beauty's castle. Inside, a prisoner had waited one hundred years for a prince to come charging in on a white horse, sword raised high. Except I wasn't a prince. And I didn't have a sword.

I had a spade.

I could feel the whispered movement, hear the magic as it retreated inwards like a tide. A soft rush of water moving in, draining towards the center. Towards the source from which it extracted life and sustenance.

I ran.

Near the walled garden room I fell, scraping clear through my jeans and bloodying my knee. Whether it had been the path that had tripped me or a give of my foot, I couldn't tell. I didn't care. The garden could have my blood. As long as it gave back what was mine.

The entrance to the walled garden was blown wide open. Grasses and weeds choked the beds, but in the middle, the diseased rose stood unchanged, reaching its ugly growth towards the blue sky.

Harmony told me a hedge witch could only work with a natural process, not against it. And what was death if not a natural process? The natural counterpoint to preservation?

If I could preserve, surely I could also destroy.

I drove my spade into the earth like it could carve out the world. I sent it down, over and over again, until I reached the root around all sides and could pry it up. I didn't have gloves—of course, I didn't have gloves—so I reached for the base of the plant, ignoring the thorns that bit my shoulders, my face, my hands. I pulled with all my weight, with all of the strength from my aching shoulders. Pain seared the skin at the inside of my wrists. My hands were already bloody from the fall, and it was excruciating. The root mass emerged inch by exasperating inch, until at last the plant came up out of the earth. It lay on its side, a diseased heap of twisted red growth. It looked less terrifying in death, and I felt only a cold, burned-out anger. Anger that the roses could demand blood and decades of care only to turn around and die so easily. Anger that they could keep a man alive for a hundred years only to abandon him at the end. The anger burned up my arms, chasing away the pain and leaving only a red-hot satisfaction. The roses would never hurt us again.

I wiped my bloody hands against my jeans and walked out into the larger garden. The air sparkled with afternoon. My hands tingled with certainty. My blood lived in these roses, alongside the water and the wine.

The roses knew me. They knew me, and they listened. Slowly, so slowly, the overgrowth beat back. The giant bushes untwisted, shrinking back to a normal size. Vines snaked away from my feet, clearing a path that led to the Temple of Aphrodite.

"Thank you," I said.

I heard a mew and looked down. Telegraph rubbed between my ankles. "Let's go, girl."

The briar roses retreated from the garden house back to where I had culled them a month ago. The steps to the house were clean and clear, and the door came easily.

"Louis!"

My voice echoed in the house. The sitting room was unoccupied, as was the kitchen. I ran upstairs just to be sure, but the bed, still tossed as though it had been recently slept in, was empty.

Telegraph waited on the front step. Of course she already knew where her person was. When she saw that I had finally cottoned on, she turned tail and led me straight to the garden folly. The not-Madame was in full bloom. It was beautiful—the pink roses were nearly fuchsia in the afternoon sunlight and they undulated gently in the breeze. I walked with confidence towards it. It remained wild, but it was mine, and I knew my roses.

Blossoms poured themselves over the lovers bench, some canes long enough to brush pink petals against the white marble. And next to the lovers bench, lying on his side in the tall grass, was Louis.

One arm curled beneath his head, his eyes closed in sleep, long eyelashes peaceful against his cheeks. He wore a white shirt with the sleeves rolled up, almost as though he meant to go foraging in the rose bushes again, but his arms were clear and unbloodied. His chest rose and fell gently.

"Louis." I knelt next to him, my knees in the grass. "Louis, wake up."

I thought again of fairytales. A prince asleep in the garden, a castle surrounded by roses. Careful not to touch him with my bloody hands, I bent over him and kissed his right temple, just where the soft hair met warm skin. I felt his pulse beneath my lips.

He stirred, grimacing, and his body curled in on itself.

"Louis," I said again. "It's me, it's Ethan. Wake up."

His eyes opened. He sat up, one hand to the grass beneath him, pushing himself slowly off the ground. He was as beautiful as I remembered. More so, in the sunlight, which revealed the thousand shades of yellow and gold in his hair. His eyes were the color of the Indiana summer sky. "Ethan."

"I'm here." I reached for him, and then remembered my bloody hands and pulled them back.

He looked at me and then around, his gaze hitching on the roses above our heads. "Ethan Keating Mendoza," he said softly. "What have you done?"

I curled my hands into fists, which did nothing to hide the scrapes that covered the backs of my hands as well. "I'm not sure. Are you alright?"

"I am now. I feel—" He looked around. "They've bloomed."

"Yes. Although they've blown, most of them."

"But not this one."

"No." Above us, the not-Madame laughed in the breeze.

"After you left." Louis hesitated. "I thought they wouldn't. Days passed, and still the buds didn't open. What day is it?"

"Saturday."

"I think the garden thought you had left for good. Without your magic it just—went. It had no reason to stay still, and so it didn't."

"You said I could leave the garden."

He looked at me quizzically. "And so you can."

"I can't," I protested. "Not if it dies without me. Not if you—" My voice broke, and I swallowed. "I dug up the sick rose. It was the only way I could think of to stop what was happening."

"It's all right."

"It isn't. Not if it means you'll die too."

He reached for my clenched hands, his thumbs pressing into my wrists until my fingers uncurled. The blood was still smeared across my palms, but the piercings were gone, and I realized the thrumming pain had vanished. He swept his thumbs over my palms, soft fingers brushing the thick calluses. "I'd say I have—oh, fifty years left. Give or take."

Telegraph inserted her head beneath my palm, pushing between us. Demanding, as always, our attention.

I laughed, stroking her perfect fur as she slinked beneath my hand. My voice sounded watery. "Now you can leave."

Louis wasn't looking at me. He was looking at the statue of Aphrodite, looming from behind the lovers bench. "My mother—in her will. She made me promise to take care of the roses. I was already estranged from the family. I hadn't spoken to her in years. She had been committed, overuse of magic. But she left her final instructions nevertheless."

"She cursed you."

"No," he said. "I cursed myself. The first few years I was so bitter, so angry at the world. I took care of the garden because it sustained me, but I didn't love it. I gave it none of myself. Not like you." His thumbs pressed into my palms, easing the pain further. "Was the money sufficient, to pay your father's debts?"

"More than. Thank you."

"But you came back."

It wasn't, quite, a question.

"Of course. I had a promise to keep."

He smiled broadly and leaned forward until his forehead touched mine. "So you did."

I closed my eyes and inhaled his chimney smoke and roses smell. "What happens now?"

"The estate will pass to—" He paused and leaned back just far enough to look into my face. "I don't know who. The county, perhaps. I don't really care. Perhaps that's terrible, given the lengths my mother went through to save it. And everything you did to make it beautiful again. But I don't." He grinned. "I don't care."

"I'm sure we can think of something wonderful for it," I said, thinking of Colonel Mustard and his penchant for guests. "And I didn't do it for the garden. I did it—well, first for the money. And then for you."

Neither of us could stop smiling. His fingers flexed in mine. "I don't know what to do now."

His face had changed yet again, lost the weight of years. He was a young man again, a man my own age, with the world before him and no idea what to make of it. He could study for the MCAT and go back to medical school, maybe. He could get a job, if he wanted one. He could ride in a truck, drink beer in a bar, bicker with my father over the rules of Clue.

We could come back to the estate, eventually, to finish what we'd started. To build something beautiful.

"Well, for starters," I said, standing up. We were still joined by our hands, and I pulled until he rose to his feet. "You can come home with me. You can help us in the rose garden until you figure out what you want to do."

His eyes searched my face, his lips parted.

"It's time you met the garden I grew up with," I said. "It's not cursed, I promise."

We made our way back out through the garden. No vines appeared to trip us as we walked across the clean-swept flagstone path. Buds surrounded us, and as we approached the main residence I heard the tell-tale sound of gravel spitting under Suzy's truck, followed by the sound of the car-door slam. "Come on," I told him. "Let's tell Suzy the good news."

He glanced down at himself, as though to remind himself of what he was wearing.

"You look fine," I said. "Men's fashions haven't changed all that much in a hundred years."

He looked horrified. "These clothes aren't a hundred years old, Christ."

I laughed at him, and then laughed with him, and when we caught our breath, he was smiling. I could see him in my mind's eye sitting at the breakfast table in my childhood home, leaning forward over a cup of coffee as my father carried on about rose care. Maybe we could take what we learned and apply it to the estate.

"Let's go," I said again.

Louis squeezed my hand, and together we made our way past the garden house. Telegraph trotted at our heels, keeping pace along the meandering flagstones, towards the drive and the old pink truck.

EPILOGUE

IN THE MIDDLE of rural north-central Indiana, between one windmill forest and another, an old house lies nestled amongst miles of corn field. Its last owners died a hundred years ago and left the property in a trust, where it remained until the last trustee petitioned to have the property donated to the county. Which eventually it was, along with a substantial donation from the same trust.

As a county-operated public park, Kilbride Gardens is an educational center and public garden dedicated to the preservation of old garden roses. The park does not charge admission, but it does operate a miniature garden center that sells propagated rose bushes, including an impressive variety of old garden roses. The property has partnered with local rosarian business Keating Mendoza Roses, who serve as advisors for the gardens and preservation initiative. Keating Mendoza Roses is credited with the re-discovery of the old garden rose *Mrs. Elizabeth Kilbride*, a delightfully cheery pink noisette, so named for the last owner and caretaker of the garden.

Though quite popular with rose aficionados, the age of the average visitor is probably about seventeen, as the spot has become increasingly popular with high school history classes, summer camps, and introductory gardening courses. The site is consequently a noisy one, rarely without visitors on any day during the warmer months. Very few of the visitors, even those who have already discovered their magic, have ever suspected anything unusual about the house itself.

And yet the house is glad, to the extent that a house can be said to show emotion. It is cheered to see the students slipping their minders, the townies satisfying their curiosity, the gardening enthusiasts in search of their new favorite flower. Tourists occasionally stumble upon the spot, venturing out on a day trip from Indianapolis in search of a little culture for the kiddos, who run about and shriek in delight the way that children do, while their parents marvel at the intricate absurdity of Victorian architecture. The house absorbs all of these moments and holds them close, because that is what a house does. It preserves.

Most of all, the house is glad when Ethan Keating Mendoza and his partner come to call, which they do in the course of their work at least several times a month. They hire a small army of talented rosarians in the summers, some of them discovered in places as unlikely as a Home Depot parking lot, others pulled from rosarian association listservs, and still others drummed up from the local high school. All of them talented enough to carry out Keating Mendoza's vision of a house dreaming through the centuries, though the pair have been careful not to restrict themselves to only those with an affinity for roses. The park employs hedge witches with talents for box hedges and bleeding heart, for oaks and weeds, for insects and decay. In the summer, the park sponsors an internship for a sommelier.

The park closes to the public at dusk, though the caretakers often stay later. Keating Mendoza and his sweetheart can sometimes be seen wandering the paths, taking stock of the day's work or simply strolling in silence. Sometimes they sit on the steps of the garden house, hand-in-hand, watching the fireflies dance up out of the grass. They never go inside. But when they wander back to the Kilbride house, they always remember to stop and say goodnight.

AUTHOR'S NOTE

THIS IS A work of fiction, and while I really do grow roses and have incorporated much of what I've learned, I also made a lot of it up. Please don't give your roses wine, no matter how bloodthirsty they seem. That said, a shot of vodka in a vase of cut flowers will extend the life of your blooms. Really.

ACKNOWLEDGMENTS

I OWE THANKS to so many people. To name just a few:

To Brianne and Josh of Shiraki Press, for their belief in Ethan and Louis' story.

To my agent, Gabrielle Harbowy, for her advice and support.

To Annie Carl, for her copyediting and expertise.

To my family, especially my husband, for their willingness to make space in our lives for my writing.

To my writing pals: Thea, Cassandra, Lezlie, Vanessa, Mike, Priya, Phil, Jasmine, Faith, Kathleen, and Terra. Without you I would be both lonelier and worse at this. Special shoutout to Beth for all the early-morning writing sessions while our kids were still sleeping, and for the many hours on the phone.

Photo by Emily O'Malley Liu

EMILY O'MALLEY LIU grew up in Palm Beach County, Florida and has lived in the American Southwest, the Midwest, New England, and Japan.

Em now resides with her husband and three kids in the greater Washington, D.C. metro area, where she researches financial systems by day and devises magic systems by night.

Wine for Roses is her first novel.

CONTRIBUTORS

Written by Emily O'Malley Liu
EMILYOMALLEYLIU.COM

Author representation by Gabrielle Harbowy
Corvisiero Literary Agency
CORVISIEROAGENCY.COM

Edited by Brianne Shiraki
SHIRAKIPRESS.COM

Front cover by Lisa Marie Pompilio
VONBROOKLYNDESIGN.COM

Book design by Josh Sutphin
SHIRAKIPRESS.COM

Sensitivity read and copy edits by Annie Carl
Annie Carl Creates
ANNIECARLAUTHOR.COM

Cover and interior artwork from Shutterstock.

This book was created entirely by humans.
No generative AI was used for any part of its production.

www.ingramcontent.com/pod-product-compliance
Lightning Source LLC
LaVergne TN
LVHW091047100526
838202LV00077B/3069